T0385412

raw content

raw content

Naomi Booth

corsair

CORSAIR

First published in Great Britain in 2025 by Corsair

1 3 5 7 9 10 8 6 4 2

A CIP catalogue record for this book is available from the British Library.

Paperback ISBN 978-1-472-15935-9

Typeset in Caslon by M Rules
Printed and bound in Great Britain by Clays Ltd, Elcograf S.p.A

Papers used by Corsair are from well-managed forests
and other responsible sources.

Corsair
An imprint of
Little, Brown Book Group
Carmelite House
50 Victoria Embankment
London EC4Y 0DZ

The authorised representative
in the EEA is
Hachette Ireland
8 Castlecourt Centre
Dublin 15, D15 XTP3, Ireland
(email: info@hbgi.ie)

An Hachette UK Company
www.hachette.co.uk

www.littlebrown.co.uk

For Lydia and Alex

For poetry makes nothing happen: it survives
In the valley of its making where executives
Would never want to tamper, flows on south
From ranches of isolation and the busy griefs,
Raw towns that we believe and die in; it survives,
A way of happening, a mouth.

W. H. AUDEN,
'In Memory of W. B. Yeats'

'Most parents now ... cannot bear their love for
their children, and all children grow up in the
light of this.'

ADAM PHILLIPS,
On Getting Better

I was born in the back of a Ford Fiesta, a mile shy of Huddersfield Royal Infirmary. As my mother screamed and my father caught me – purple and larded with vernix – in his shaking hands, Jacqueline Hill's body was being uncovered in the thick of nettles and dock and ragwort on a scrap of wasteland twenty miles away. She had disappeared the night before, becoming the final victim of the Yorkshire Ripper.

I was born in the Colne Valley, into a seam of abandoned mills. The landscape of my childhood was Salendine Nook and Scarbottom and Titanic Mills. Derelict furnace chimneys and saw-tooth roofs were as intrinsic to the valley as the skylarks and meadow pipits that rose in the sky above us to the Pennine moortops.

I grew up in a house ten miles, as the crow flies, from Saddleworth Moor, where children lay buried under gorse and heather in unmarked graves – if the crow were to fly up over Marsden Moor and Wessenden Reservoir, to the forbidden and terribly beautiful places: to Dovestones Edge and the Boggart Stones.

My childhood was a map marked with danger zones. Titanic

Mills, filled with broken glass and pigeon shit, in which we were forbidden to play. The lanes and ginnels and car parks that run behind old coal yards and pubs, in which we were forbidden to play. The secluded crescents of greenspace next to the canal where people dumped old sofas and chest freezers and tins of paint, in which we were forbidden to play. Even the playground at the edge of our estate was to be accessed only in specific circumstances. It had to be daylight; it had to be before seven in the evening; we were not to speak to strangers; me and my sister must always stick together. We were never, ever, to wander away from the playground into the woods, where people sniffed glue and worse. We were never, ever to walk up towards Scapegoat Hill or Marsden Moor.

Me and my sister were cared for. We were bathed and fed and clothed. But, as with many children, we couldn't have told you if we were loved. Our experience of care came in the form of a warning.

<glitch>

My work requires me to be careful. For approximately nine hours each day, I sit in the same position, my ankles crossed as I lean over my keyboard. The desks in our office are arranged in rows, partitioned with prefabricated dividers, and twenty-three other people work alongside me, sitting in approximately the same position – though some have ergonomic chairs and wrist supports and footstools. I manage a small team of editors and our caseloads. Tariq, who sits next to me, is in daily disarray. He edits his cases in hard copy and papers cover his desk and most of the floor around it. His workstation is close to being a fire hazard. Tariq's wife is agoraphobic, and he receives regular calls from her and from the school that his children attend. I speak to his wife sometimes, if Tariq is away from his desk; she sobs down the line if a delivery driver has knocked at her door, and I usually fail to soothe her. Lucy sits on the other side of me: she commutes in from Leeds and, most mornings, is catatonically hungover. She sometimes naps in the stock cupboard. In the afternoons, she ingests Ritalin and listens to techno on her headphones to sharpen her up enough for casework. I pretend not to know any of this: Tariq and Lucy always get their work done, and I have no desire to interfere with their relationships or substance dependencies. Most of the people in our office have ended up working in legal publishing by unhappy accident. There are people like me, who had fancy notions of working with books, but had no 'in' with the literary publishing houses in London. There are law graduates, like Lucy, who didn't make it to the end of their training. And there are ex-solicitors, like Tariq, who have been forced out of the profession by the terrible training pay and hours that are impossible to manage alongside family life.

December. There's been a hard freeze for days. Lucy types away next to me in fingerless gloves. It's been down to minus seven at night; in the daytime, it hasn't risen above zero for a week. People complain about the cold as we work, and about the groaning office boiler. Our office, the Granary, is a converted agricultural building in a village on the outskirts of York: an attempt at a regional presence, which also happens to be much cheaper than expanding the London offices. As well as the Editorial and Production teams, the Granary houses a colony of bats, hidden in the old wooden rafters, which Estates tell us cannot be legally removed. Bats are a protected species. Every so often, a creature drops, folded like a secret letter, on to the desk of someone in our team and will either be swept into a bin or woken by the human who is screaming at it. That doesn't happen in the London office, where the windows gleam and I've never seen so much as a wasp.

I moved to York more than a decade ago. I live in a flat on the fifth floor of a new-build block, overlooking a supermarket car park and then the ring road and the edge of the city – cars, pedestrians, cyclists, flowing in and out under the crenellated city walls. When I first moved into this flat, replete with thick, beige carpets and rental furniture and anonymous artworks, I had the strangest thought: I imagined hurling myself out of this high window. I looked out, through the branches of a tall lime tree, to the car park below and saw a body, face down; then a forensic tent erected around it. I briefly thought I would have to move out. But I discovered that the windows hinged outwards, and that it was only possible to open them by a couple of inches, and the thought stopped bothering me.

This December, when I look out of my flat, the supermarket roof and the top of the city wall are the same dazzling white, the skyline monochrome with frost. When I walk around the ring road to my bus stop, the tarmac is dulled with salt and grit. The freeze descends from broken guttering and overflowing outlet pipes, down exterior walls and across pavements in spills of bottle ice. But the frost also seems to rise up – from objects that you'd never think would freeze. A child's pink glove, dropped on the pavement, has cultured a layer of frost, delicate as mould.

I imagine the glove cordoned off by police tape.

I often see the world like this: as a crime scene in waiting.

My bus ride takes me out of the city. Buildings give way to fields, which flooded back in the autumn, and have frozen over now. Pylons erupt from swathes of glittering ice, like prehistoric creatures from a frozen sea. I continue to travel to work through the freeze, despite strangers – including the man who works at the Co-op in the village – shouting at me to be careful. Here he is again, leaving his post to call out to me: Watch yourself, love! It's bad on that corner this morning. You don't want to risk a slip now, eh.

Many a slip twixt cup and lip. My nan's favourite warning when anyone dared to express optimism.

I don't register the cold – or much else – once I'm immersed in my work. Everyone in the Cases Team must work at speed; the law is changing with each new judgment and it's our job to make sure new precedents are discoverable online. We are sent the raw content of cases, and then we must edit it, applying the correct metadata tags so that the cases can be submitted to our Content Management System. If I am working on a case for the European Court of Justice, I will tag the sections as follows: *<Case name>; <Application number>; <Judges>; <The facts>; <JUDGMENT>*. Within these parent sections, I'll introduce numerous child- or subsections: *<The circumstances of the case>; <Relevant domestic law >; <Alleged violations>*, etc. Once I've completed the tagging hierarchy for a case, I'll scan the text again, making sure there are no anomalies and that the text will appear cleanly on a screen. Then I'll amend the grammar and formatting. I'll create lists of other cases referred to. I'll insert hyperlinks to relevant previous case law. I'll add and remove italics, I'll insert bullet points, I'll add numbers to the paragraphs. I scan the content again, barely reading it. I tidy up words that, in other contexts, outside of our Content Management System, are records of devastation: *Her detention was not lawful . . . Extradition was not conducted with due diligence . . . Expulsion had put him at risk of ill-treatment . . . When the applicant returned home, she discovered the bodies of her husband and son . . .*

Our work is detail-oriented, but it must be completed urgently – legal practitioners and defendants are waiting for it – which means that, despite its technical nature, I find it absorbing. When I first learned how to work in XML, I had to practise tagging dummy documents for days on end. One night, while I was completing this training, I dreamt of a working day formed of hierarchised sections. In the dream, I woke in the root element *<working day>*. I travelled to work, and my ride on the bus to the village was contained in the subsection *<journey>*. And within this *<journey>*,

I entered another subsection: *<bus> <transaction with driver>* in which I fumbled for money and paid for a day return *</transaction with driver>*. The dream became increasingly anxious: if I didn't complete all the closing tags, I would be left suspended in a day that could never parse or close. I'd be trapped in an endless sequence of glitches and error warnings.

I've been employed in this office for more than ten years. I have worked my way up from Editorial Assistant to Assistant Editor to Editor to Senior Editor and now to Cases Team Leader. I am being groomed for divisional leadership. When I'm working, I am absorbed by house style rules and metatags and our Content Management System and by the design and application of work flows for my team. The top drawer of my desk is a mess of defunct biros and post-its, beneath which is my stash of paracetamol-with-caffeine and Reese's Pieces. In combination, drugs and sugar enable me to work to deadline through hunger and discomfort. This winter, I am working at a suboptimal distance from my screen: my right shoulder is sore and the sinews in my neck are too tender to touch. I have to take paracetamol every few hours. I have been invited several times to have a new workstation assessment. I should also have been assessed for lone late-night working. But taking up the offer of these assessments would be to admit that something significant is actually happening to me: that the bump in front of me, which is increasing my distance from my monitor and the suboptimal angle of my arms to my workstation, is in fact a growing human infant.

I struggle to say the word *pregnant* aloud. I lower my voice when I am required to say it in a meeting with HR. I feel embarrassed by it. *I'm pregnant.* I say it as though I'm in a confession box.

I sit at my desk, seven and a half months *pregnant*, working diligently through my cases, refusing to prepare for the arrival of the baby. I have bought nothing for her. And Ryan – I don't even know what to call him. My boyfriend. My partner. My co-parent. None of these terms feels right for Ryan – a man significantly younger than me, whom I have been dating for just short of a year, who is about to move from London to my one-bedroom rental in York in readiness for our baby's alleged arrival.

I met Ryan at our work Christmas party the December before the long freeze. I used to regularly attend training and events at the 'mothership' – our London office on Liverpool Street. It was difficult for Tariq to get away, so I often covered his meetings in London too, which I liked doing. When I went down to London, I was taken out by the commissioning editors and the marketing team to bougie nightclubs in Kensington and locals in East London. On one of my first trips down, Nadia, the Editorial Divisional Manager, took me out to a pub in Leytonstone and then back to her flat, where her flatmate, a trainee chef at a Michelin-starred restaurant, cooked snails for us that he had foraged in Hackney Marshes. We ate together in their tiny living room, drinking white wine from bright plastic cups. The snails were gristly and pungent, but I worked my way through them. I wanted to sample everything that London had to offer. I woke the next morning on Nadia's sofa in unfamiliar pyjamas and I was sick in her shower. But I smartened myself up by the time of my morning meeting with an eminent barrister back in central London. My first ever meeting with an author. I didn't know that, back then, the barristers were even worse than the commissioning editors: they often used to order wine with lunch and things could get messy. This one took my hand and told me I reminded him of a long-ago girlfriend who had skin that was speckled with freckles like an egg; I tried to steer him back towards his contracted manuscript and when I might expect it to be delivered.

Our Christmas party was held in a pub in Spitalfields. The company had hired the whole venue, splashing out with a buffet of Thai street food on the ground floor; a 'chill-out' space on the first floor with a live acoustic guitarist; and up on the top floor, a DJ. The whole group of us, minus Tariq, travelled down together from the York office. We were drunk before we left the hotel. We had the reckless energy of teenagers out on the lash, and London knew it: commissioning editors and marketing execs swooped in on the dance floor, provided bumps of coke. Married production crew were necking senior London managers before 10 p.m.

I watched the tinselly carnage unfolding. I drank shots at the free bar and I danced and I shouted along to the music, but I wasn't as hammered as the rest of them. Or I wasn't drunk in the right way: I exited the slurry, messy jubilance of the dance floor.

Downstairs, in the chill-out space, I sat with a new starter who was weeping; she kept apologising, saying she didn't know why she was crying. Christmas songs always made her like this, she said, since she had lost her mum. The new starter had a good sob on my shoulder, then went off to repair her face in the loo.

The acoustic guitarist was playing 'White Christmas': his Bublé-style version slowed at the end into something more complex; a broken chord that lingered. I found myself staying to listen to him. The girl who'd been crying had recovered – she emerged from the toilets, face re-sheened with make-up, and pointed to show me she was going upstairs to dance. I waved her off.

Maybe the thought of Christmas was making me maudlin too. I had last seen my mum, briefly, the Christmas before: we had both had too much to drink, and my mum wept as we parted, as she often does, apologising to me: *I'm sorry, Grace, I'm sorry. I didn't ever mean for things to be like this.*

The party was into its final half-hour. People were peeling off – into corners together, back to hotel rooms, on to the night bus. I watched the guitarist play his last song: his total concentration, the way he oriented his body around his guitar. He was young and gangly, but his hands moved with intense dexterity.

He caught my gaze as he looked up from his final song, scanning the room, hopeful for applause, perhaps.

I clapped and then surprised myself by whooping – so maybe I was a little drunk, after all.

I've finished for the night, the guitarist said a few moments later, sitting down next to me with his pint. I'd offer to buy you a drink. But I guess it doesn't count for much when the bar's free? I'm Ryan, by the way.

He was handsome and almost cocky, Ryan-by-the-way. But he couldn't make eye contact with me and he was playing with a beer mat as he spoke. He was pretending confidence. Method acting.

I liked hearing you play, I said.

It's decent of you to listen, he said. Most people don't. Not once they've had a few drinks. At this point in the evening, you usually get hecklers or groups of pissed girls who want to sing along.

I asked him if he did a lot of corporate parties, and he told me about his Christmas season so far: five gigs a week since the start of November. This week he'd played for estate agents and micro-brewers and web designers and now—

Fuck, I've forgotten. He laughed. No offence, but what is it you do again?

We're legal publishers, I said. We edit and publish legal cases online when a judgment's delivered.

Sounds interesting, he said.

It mostly isn't, I said. It's mostly maritime and tort law – long cases on legal responsibility and negligence. Occasionally you do get something grisly though. Criminal law reports. Or the European Court of Human Rights. People seem to think the European Court system is all about mandating the curve of bananas, since the referendum campaign. But it really isn't. It's more likely to be dealing with a woman in Chechnya discovering her son buried in her own back garden by Russian militants.

Fucking hell, he said. That's dark.

I might have killed the mood now. Chatting about atrocity and European law isn't what everyone wants in the dying moments of a Christmas party.

Ryan knocked back his pint. He drank like someone who was used to being on a timed break. He glanced at me, then scanned the room again. He didn't quite know what to do with himself. He reminded me of the sharpest lads I went to school with, who smoked skunk to blunt their energy and appetites and were often struck dumb as a result. Ryan was restless and hard to read in the same young, magnetic way.

I told him that I lived in York, that I was just down in London for the night. He told me he was originally from Bristol, and that he was living on a houseboat on the Thames.

When we'd finished our drinks, he stared at the floor and asked if he could walk me back to my hotel.

Not if you live on a boat, I said. I want to see it.

We take a night bus, then follow cobbled streets down towards the river. We are close to Tower Bridge, Ryan tells me: we'll see it in a moment and then I'll have my bearings. There are small restaurants and pubs tucked away on these side streets, all of them closed now, but the lights in one reveal a lone worker cashing up; in another, two colleagues downing shots together.

It is almost 1 a.m. It is bitterly cold. I hear the river before I can see it: a clean, rhythmical, tidal whoosh. Clinking metal. I feel the sting of frost in my fingertips and lips. My pulse flickers against the raw night air through my nipples, tongue, clitoris. Intoxication makes me feel embodied – vital, totally sensitised – and detached at the same time. I am watching myself follow a stranger down a cobbled path towards dark water. My body throbs with anticipation.

Flash of a future crime scene: my bare limbs strobing through dark water.

Ryan unlocks a gate, which opens on to a walkway above the river.

Be careful, he says. The light's not too good. Here, I'll go ahead and you hold my hand.

The walkway moves underfoot. It's connected to a network of ramshackle platforms, which serve as moorings for several boats. The boats are like mini-tankers – not at all the diminutive canal barges I have been picturing. The Thames is below us. On the opposite bank of the river: a block of luxury flats that looks, at first glance, like a towering cruise ship. When we're further out on the walkway, Tower Bridge appears, massive, on our left, lit up in blue and white.

This is fucking unreal, I say.

It's fucking cold is what it is, Ryan says. Are you sure about this? I've got to warn you that I live with two boys. And the electricity sometimes cuts out, which means we can't always flush the loo. Like I said, the boat's really basic.

I'm game, I say.

Ryan's bedroom is a small cabin. His bed is a bunk, with a desk and storage space built in beneath it. I climb up to his mattress using the ladder and find myself so close to the ceiling that I have to lie down immediately. We kiss and it is awkward in the small space. The boat creaks in the water as we move back and forth and back and forth. The noise of clinking all around us. In the darkness, my senses are totally alive. To the rocking and the clinking and to the smells of the boat: damp wood, a faint vegetal odour from the toilet pump, the salt of Ryan's skin.

In the morning, I climb down from the bed and fall straight over.

Morning, Ryan says, laughing – a deep, liquid gurgle. Watch yourself. It's low tide. We're on the mud now, so the boat's on a tilt.

I bump into Ryan's boatmate, Larry, on my way to the loo, and he tells me I must not use a hairdryer while on the boat.

One girl did that before, he says to me, sorrowfully, and it shorted the electrics.

Thank you for warning me, I say. I didn't pack a hairdryer.

Larry nods – his fear of a woman wielding her electrical appliances abated – and retreats to his cabin.

*

After that night, whenever I had a meeting in London, I would find my way back to Ryan's boat. Being there was a full-body experience: the wash of the tide, the closeness of the cabin, the metallic scent of the water, the tacky warmth of Ryan's body, the organic tang of his skin, the way his orgasm surged so quickly, seeming to surprise even him. I lost myself there as if underwater for long stretches – pleasure extending me into the coldest depths, my imagination flashing to limbs strobing in the dark, until my whole body throbbed and ebbed with the undertow.

Each time I visited Ryan, it took me a while to get accustomed to the boat's lulling – and then a while again to adapt to the stasis of the pavement. When your body has accommodated the rhythm of the water, climbing back on earth stops you short before making you reel.

When spring arrived, the boats on the jetty erupted into colour – boxes of daffodils, exteriors repainted in peppermint and cerise, sky and river filling with light again. I felt woozy for days on end. And I thought: maybe I've adjusted to the water so completely that I'm no longer steady on dry land.

One evening back in York, in the pub after work, the wine that I've ordered tastes unexpectedly harsh.

I think it's corked, I say. I push my glass away.

Give it here, Lucy says to me. That bottle's probably just been open too long. She takes a swig. Shrugs. Tastes fine to me, she says.

I don't track my cycle. I don't track anything outside of my work. Every few weeks, my period arrives as a bloody surprise. I try to think back to when I last bought tampons: I remember it was still cold. And now we are sitting outside and there is light in the sky at 8 p.m.; it's the cusp of summer. The penny drops: it occurs to me to take a pregnancy test.

I don't tell Ryan straight away. I harbour these illicit, roiling sensations for a few days longer. I feel like I'm stoned: blithely disoriented, low-level nauseated, waking dry-mouthed in the middle of the night and craving fresh, sour fruit.

When I do tell Ryan, it is in a Pizza Express close to King's Cross station, just before I'm due to board the train back to York. I've been trying to tell him all day; now the words spill out of me at the last possible moment.

I'm pregnant.

The conversation glitches. My own voice far away.

Ryan shakes his head several times. He tells me he needs a minute. He stands up; goes to the toilet. When he comes back to our table, he holds my hand in his. I have to stop myself from laughing when he says the word *baby*. He pauses just before he utters it. His Adam's apple bobs before saying that word – *baby* – as though he might be stopping himself from vomiting.

He says it is up to me what we do with the – *um, baby* – and he'll support whatever I want.

But I am disinclined to *do* anything.

Is curiosity a sufficient reason to continue with a pregnancy? That is what I remember feeling: a reckless curiosity about what would happen next.

Being pregnant feels like accepting a lift from a stranger; it's like stepping into a stolen car and leaning back as it accelerates: thrilling, in part, because it could be totally fucking disastrous. I am joyriding to somewhere unknown, and I don't feel afraid, not at first – I abdicate responsibility to whatever is happening inside me.

Ryan and his things arrive in a van a week before Christmas. I am sitting at my kitchen table waiting for him and triaging my inbox, then making a list of what I'll need to prioritise in the weeks before my maternity leave. I begin to draft a job description for the internal secondment to cover my role. When the intercom buzzes, my first instinct is to ignore it. When it buzzes again, I picture myself pulling the box off the wall.

On the small black-and-white video screen in my hallway, I watch the torso of a man in a hoodie moving in and out of shot. It's all been a misunderstanding, I want to shout into the speaker. False alarm! Sorry! You can go back to your boat now!

Ryan and his van-driving friend, Max, unload boxes and sports bags full of clothes into my hallway, along with two guitars and an amp. I make myself a cup of tea and keep out of the way. I look out of my bedroom window – the sky is cold and colourless over the Sainsbury's car park today. Has the baby moved since I woke? At my last appointment, the midwife told me I should be tracking the baby's movements every day, to get a sense of a normal pattern. When I'm at work, I usually fail to do this. Imagine pulling up in the middle of a meeting to note down that something has just stirred inside you at 11.37 a.m. I find it hard to connect what I've seen on the screen at the ultrasounds – cluster of tiny organs, grainy shapes of foetal life flickering in uterine darkness – with the idea of a real, living infant. Perhaps I can't track these movements because trawling my internal sensations for loss feels too much like tempting fate.

Ryan and Max are hugging in the hallway and then hammering each other's backs.

Look after him, Max says to me. He's one of the good ones.

Ryan and I stand in the hall and watch Max go. We haven't touched one another yet. Ryan leans in around the bump and gives me a wet kiss on my neck.

Shall we go out for a drink or something? he says. I can make a start on the boxes tomorrow?

It's dusk when we leave the flat, and the afternoon darkens quickly, the light dropping like a stone. Almost midwinter. York is dressed for Christmas – the old, narrow streets in the city centre laced with white and blue bulbs, the bare trees dripping with them too. Men and women stagger out of pubs, coatless, faces illuminated by spirits and sequins. My mind flashes forward to the early hours, to the crime-scene aftermath of the festivities: an empty alleyway, broken pint glass, blood spattered on the wall.

All the bars and pubs and restaurants are rammed, so we go to a hot chocolate stall at the Christmas market.

Ryan orders a double Cointreau with his and asks if I'd like a shot. He quickly corrects himself: Oh, course not. Sorry. Unless you do want one? I'm not choosing for you. It's up to you. Obviously.

It's fine, I say. I'll have the classic.

Are you OK, he asks, walking around instead of sitting? We could try to find a bench?

It's good to move around, I say.

Right, OK, he says.

Then we fall into silence.

We don't know what to say to each other. Fucking hell. I can't think of a single thing to say to him. We bypassed the minutiae of first dates, went straight to weekends pressed close together on the boat, and then straight into baby panic-planning. For weeks, for months, all we've talked about is what we should *do*, and then, how we should do it – whether Ryan should move to be closer to me and the baby (he wanted to, he said, he wanted to step up and be proper hands on, though he looked stricken as he said it), then whether we should live together (no-brainer – Ryan would have no income when he first moved up and he has no savings), then when he'd move to York. Now that he's here, it feels ridiculous to ask him basic auto-biographical questions. What was he like at school? When did he learn to play guitar? How does he vote? Does he even vote? Are there things that run in his family – like diabetes or male-pattern baldness or religious impulses? I should have asked these questions long ago.

Ryan breaks the silence to tell me he's got an interview to-morrow. He tells me about a new coffee shop that's opening on Fossgate. He's done barista work before, he says, when he first moved to London, so it should be OK. He'll start off with that, and then look for regular gigs and guitar teaching. Maybe tap into the local wedding scene.

I'd like to meet your family, he says. Before, you know. Too long.

I tell him that my dad and his wife, Lillian, are keen to visit – next weekend maybe.

What about your mum?

Not my mum, I say. She's . . . it's delicate.

Oh, yeah, Ryan says. You said you don't see her much?

The truth is, I've only just told my mother about the pregnancy. I did it the coward's way: via text message – *Hi Mum, I've got some news. Sorry to be telling you so late.*

My mother had started a reply – I could see that she was typing. But she abandoned whatever she was trying to say, and the message thread has gone cold.

We reach the neck of the Shambles – the narrow, medieval street that tourists always photograph. It's unusually quiet. Christmas lights glimmer on the old timber frames.

Fucking hell, Ryan says, this is proper beautiful. Let's walk down here?

Yeah, sure, I say, but you'll need to give me your arm.

My ankles are unreliable under my new weight: cobbles are chancy now.

Ryan slides his arm around my waist. We pass shut-up shops selling fudge and Harry Potter merchandise, Whitby jet and speciality teas. We pass the house of the martyr Margaret Clitherow, who was pressed to death, heavy with child, under her own front door. I tell Ryan about the street: it was once the butchering district, the Great Flesh Shambles. The lane dips in the middle because that is where the offal and run-off from open-air slaughter used to be discarded. This is often called the most picturesque street in Britain, but whenever I glimpse the Shambles, deserted in the moonlight like this, I always catch something moving in the darkness at the edge of my vision; a swill of viscera down the black cobbles; the remainder of ancient violence.

*

We are easier with one another by the time we approach my flat, chatting, and then kissing on the street corner. Ryan's saliva – sugary and copious – is a shock to me. I'm super-aware of the mechanics of the kiss: the muscle of his tongue, the movement of his jaw. I really haven't kissed that much while sober.

Once we're back inside the flat, we both go quiet again.

Perhaps I should treat it like an ordinary Tuesday night, brush my teeth and take off my make-up. Or I should try to make out with Ryan, as if it is a weekend back in the early days on the boat.

We stand together in the hallway with the bump between us again. It's extraordinary, still, to glance down and see this great dome of flesh and water and soft new bones.

Ryan offers to sleep on the sofa. It'll take me a while to wind down, he says, and I know you've got work. I might just head to Sainsbury's first and get something to drink. Fetch some supplies.

OK, I say.

So, can I, like, have a key? he says.

Of course. Sorry, I say. I fish around in a drawer in the hall table and give him a spare.

I wake in the middle of the night. There's whimpering somewhere in the darkness. The cry of a wordless child – dumb, helpless mewl of pain – clarifies into mumbling. Ryan. I live with a Ryan now. Ryan's on his phone. I hear him as I pass the living room on my way to the bathroom. He's laughing, that low, liquid gurgle, then shushing himself: Nah, stop it. I know. It's crazy. It's mad. Stop it. You're cracking me up, mate, and I need to be quiet – Nah, it's not like that. I'm excited, man. Honestly. Don't let that dickhead get too comfortable in my cabin, though. He's only subletting.

I lived with a man once before in this flat: my ex-boyfriend, Sol. I haven't told Ryan about this yet. It was a short-lived attempt at cohabitation: we managed just shy of two months together. Sol had been friends with my sister, Isobel, at school, but I hadn't bothered to distinguish him within the group of lads Isobel always had around her, who were addressed by corrupted surnames or other monikers of mysterious provenance: Wardy and Twig and Stash and Hooky. Sol and I only got together years later, when I was back in the valley to meet Isobel at the pub on Christmas Eve, and Sol was there too, with that bunch of pseudonymous lads. He'd been living abroad, he told me over a pint, working at an orphanage in Porto and getting his Portuguese up to scratch. His face was tanned. He wore a T-shirt even though it was December, and his forearms were thick and sun-golden too and worked over with black tattoos. Sol had done an Open University course, he told me, and was trying to get translation work now. He wanted to translate books, but he'd settle for anything in the meantime. He was only back home while he applied for jobs, he kept saying, he was only back here for a bit.

We went outside together, Sol and I. I was jittery with cold and alcohol. The valley was black and deep around us, and I could hear the wind tunnelling up the valleyside, up Scapegoat Hill, then scouring across the moortops. Someone was playing guitar inside the pub, and Sol's mouth was warm and deep, and we sank into each other that night, in the alleyway at the side of the pub. *I've been in love with you for so long*, he said to me later. *Did you know?* I had not known. I had thought that every lad in that group was secretly in love with Isobel.

When Sol came to live with me in York, it was wild and wonderful and we were all over each other all the time. Even a trip to Sainsbury's felt like crossing a wild new frontier together. We bought pans and then we didn't use them: we couldn't make a meal together without falling on to each other, eating each other up. And then I needed space to breathe – just a little bit, Sol – and then he pushed harder, wanted more of me, and I was gasping for air, and he was wounded and resentful, and then he was disappearing into the Groves to score, and I was wrung out with worry: both of us consumed and overwhelmed by the other.

I never wanted to live like that again.

Ever since Sol, my relationships have been brief: one-night stands that sour by morning, or chats on the apps that fizzle out or quickly cloy into claustrophobia.

Cohabiting with Ryan is different. We talk about safe, procedural things, like meals and Ryan's shift patterns and who will go to the shops. We are careful with one another. We are respectful of each other's possible need for space and privacy. Perhaps this is what relationships are like if you understand what boundaries are.

We hardly touch one another.

Ryan starts work at the coffee shop the day after his

interview – and when he gets home, he tells me how knackered
he is. He yawns and stretches his neck.

I'm knackered too, I say. And then I roll my shoulders and mime
the achiness of my body.

It is true that I am tired: it is hard to sleep now; hard to get
comfy around the new limbs that are forming inside me. But we
are also performing our knackeredness to each other. Too knackered to talk; too knackered to make out; too knackered to think
about the future and what's about to happen to us both.

We eat together each evening, then Ryan plays guitar for a
while, then he moves on to video games to unwind. He does this
in the bedroom, so that I can have the living room to myself – there
is always some piece of work for me to finish off or something I
need to check before the next morning – and then, when I'm tired,
we swap places: Ryan moves into the living room and I go to bed.
I scroll on my phone and listen to what Ryan might be doing. I
sleep fitfully. Noises from the night outside infiltrate my dreams.
A mewling fox becomes a baby keening in the darkness, crying
all hours of the day and night, the neighbours are banging on the
walls until I turn on the nightlight and the crying recedes back
into the distant scream of fox.

Ryan's body clock is different from mine: he's calibrated to late
nights and the adrenaline wave of performance. He finds it hard
to accept it when I tell him that, no, he's right, there really isn't
anywhere to get a decaf coffee in York after 7 p.m. He sometimes
leaves the flat suddenly late at night to walk off his energy. Or
he goes down to the supermarket car park to smoke and pace
around. But he's fine, he says. He's OK, he's just getting used to
a 9-to-5. He could do with finding someone to score some weed
from; that'll help with the evenings. When he says this, he rasps

his thumb against the wheel of his lighter again and again. The sound scratches through to my nerves. That almost spark. My mind glitches on the memory of a case report: the sound of flame singeing into soft flesh.

I take Ryan to meet my sister, Isobel, in that frantic week before Christmas when men go out in packs, wearing novelty jumpers and violently drinking away half their December wage. We travel by train to Huddersfield as rain and sleet lash the TransPennine line. We are keeping it simple: a drink in the pub at the station. I know what works with Isobel: anything too formal, anything that requires a precise time of arrival – like a meal in a restaurant, for example – is off the cards. I message Isobel as we board the train: *Have you left yet?? GET ON THE BUS RIGHT NOW, ISOBEL.* Even so, she is almost an hour late to meet us, and when she arrives, she is talking even faster than usual, hugging Ryan hard, spilling the contents of her bag on to the pub table to try to find her lighter, revealing a miscellany of lipsticks and loose change and loose pills and tampons and baggies, and then careering round the pub to ask for a light.

I apologise to Ryan for Isobel's lateness and for her chaos.

Don't worry, he says, I'll go find her and get a round in. What do you fancy?

Another soda and lime, I guess, I say. And more crisps.

Ryan retrieves Isobel, and I watch them do a shot of something together at the bar before they come back to the table with a dark ale for Ryan, a double vodka tonic for Iz, and my pointless drink.

I approve, Isobel says to me. I know you've been waiting for my blessing. Ha! I challenged him to a shot of Unicum and he actually followed through. So, I hereby approve of this young lad becoming the father of my niece. Actually, how young are you, Ryan?

When Ryan tells her he's twenty-four, Isobel snorts. Fucking hell! Grace, you cradle snatcher.

Isobel is on a roll now. She goes on to tell us about the most disgusting drink ever brewed, which is made from stag semen, which she tried once at a house party in Saddleworth, which was actually a fucking awful house party, because Kat and Steve had lured people with novelty drinks but there was no sound system, so people drank them dry and then went on into Manchester, which was pretty bad manners, but understandable in the circumstances, right, because who throws a party without music, that's a kind of torture, because without music it's all just boring yammer yammer yammer about craft beer and music producers, actually, I really need a fag – and then Isobel is gone again.

About half an hour later, Isobel is still outside and I have had it. I can't use alcohol to lift my mood now and I've no stamina for long sessions and the sober discomfort of bench-seats. I need to eat something other than crisps. Isobel's night will escalate from here; mine's already nosedived.

I think we should go home, I say to Ryan.

Already? Ryan says. But—

Then he stops himself.

Yeah, sure, sorry, of course. Let's head back.

*

We find Isobel out on the front steps of the train station, chatting and smoking with two older women who are wearing pink fluffy reindeer antlers.

When Isobel sees me, she gawps.

Fucking hell, Grace, she says. You really *are* pregnant!

We've got to go, Iz, I say. I'm not up to a long session.

But you've only just arrived! Come on, Gracie. Come on. Ryan, talk some sense into my sister. Who knows when the two of you'll next get to go out together, eh? Well, if you're really going, I'll just have to settle in for a drink with my good friends Karen and Clare here.

Later that night, Isobel messages me: *Don't get mad with me but we had to call a fucking ambulance for Karen! The dizzy cow had never had a sherbet dab b4 and thought she was having a heart attack??!!*

A high proportion of Isobel's nights out end with the arrival of an ambulance or a police car.

I tell Ryan that Isobel has probably given one of those women her first ever line of speed and then the woman has had a panic attack.

Ha, Ryan says. She's good craic, your sister.

He stares longingly out of the window of the flat and then looks back down at his phone.

On Christmas Eve, I put on my out-of-office and then we head into town to meet my dad, Patrick, and his wife, Lillian.

What's he like, then, Ryan asks, as we walk towards the city centre.

Well, I say, he's in the police. He *was* in the police. From being seventeen. He took early retirement about five years ago.

OK, says Ryan. But what's he *like*? You've said the word *police* a lot of times. It's making me nervous.

It's a good question. What is my father like? I always struggle to describe the people closest to me; it's like trying to sense how your own mouth tastes.

He's tall, I tell Ryan. And disappointed.

Disappointed in what? Ryan asks.

Everything, I say. And everyone. My mother, who left when I was nine. My sister, obviously. He doesn't speak to her. He spent his whole life in the police, surrounded by the worst kind of stuff. Thank fuck for Lillian. They got married just before he retired and – well, you'll see. Nothing can bring Lillian down.

We pass under the city walls and into the heart of town where people are already screaming merry and stumbling into one another.

At the restaurant they seat us in the window, where we have an excellent view of the drunken parties staggering on the street outside.

Lillian says: This reminds me of your Saturday-night shifts, Pat, love. What did you used to call it? The piss patrol.

The piss patrol? Ryan says. He's trying with my dad, asking questions, despite my dad's baleful manner. What's that then?

My father takes his time responding. Swills his pint. He seems to find it hard to look at Ryan.

Then he explains that on weekends he used to have to send his lads down the side streets in the centre of town, looking for drunk-and-disorderlies. Deploying officers to look for folk pissing against walls. That's what they call *community policing*, he says. It's what I used to call the piss patrol.

What a joke, Lillian says. You're well off out of it, Pat, love.

I am, he says. I am.

Dad lapses back into silence. Lillian tells us that they are off to Greece at Easter, that they are going to stay on an island in one of those hotels with lots of different restaurants to choose from in the evenings, that the hotel has three different pools, and they could never have done a thing like that and gone away for a fortnight when Patrick was still in the force.

We've ordered sherry and tapas. I'm going to allow myself one small glass, a 25cl measure of fino, just to take the edge off.

Good on you, love, Lillian says. You deserve a little treat!

When the waiter sets my glass down, he tells me that it's made from Palomino grapes, and that it is young and deliciously sour.

I sip the drink. It tastes cold and toxic. I picture the substance moving into my bloodstream, plugging straight into my placenta. And then I can't drink any more.

I pass it to over to Ryan and he knocks it back like a shot.

Everyone is on their best behaviour – I am trying to seem content in the manner of a beatific pregnant woman; Ryan is trying to seem affable and responsible; my dad is – well, he's here, at least; Lillian is trying to constrain herself to polite lines of questioning, but after a while she can't keep from asking: So, what is it you're doing for work again, Ryan? The baby's just going to sleep in your room to start with, is she, and then you'll want to think about a bit more space, won't you?

At the end of the evening, we're back out on the pavement and my father shakes hands with Ryan.

It's good to meet you, Ryan says to him.

Likewise, my dad says, though I can see that he's looking over Ryan's shoulder, right past him towards something that is taking place in the back of a taxi over the road.

I move in to hug my dad, but he holds me back by my elbows.

Careful, Grace, he says to me, as though even a hug is a reckless activity at this point in pregnancy. You take care of yourself. He kisses me goodbye on the cheek.

Ryan and I walk back towards the flat, the noise and light of town dying behind us.

I'm sorry my dad was so dour, I say to Ryan.

He's pretty intimidating, Ryan says. I had to stop myself from calling him *sir*.

Ha, I say. Sorry. He hasn't always been quite as bad as this.

I wonder then if I should tell Ryan more. If he googles my father's name, for example, if he reads about my father in the press, then it might look like I've tried to hide something from him.

There was this case, I say to Ryan. A bad one. A few years ago. That's why he retired. It kind of finished him off. It was national news.

I never watch the news, Ryan says. It's too depressing. What was this case then? Anything I'd have heard of?

Well, I say, it was eight years ago now—

I stop and do the maths. Eight years ago, Ryan would have been sixteen. He won't have heard of the Baby S case. He would have been a child himself.

Three women are sitting on a wall outside the dodgy pub closest to my flat, drinking and vaping. 'Last Christmas' is spilling out of the pub doorway.

Merry fucking Christmas! the women shout as we pass.

Merry fucking Christmas! Ryan shouts back.

W hat is my father like?

Here you are, at ten years old, following your father down the steep roads of the estate, Isobel trailing behind you. People look twice at our father as we pass by. Children playing in front gardens go quiet. Kids making mischief in a phone box scatter. Everyone on the estate, everyone in the whole valley, seems to know that our father is police. But perhaps they would stare whether he was police or not. He is an enormous man. His nose has been broken more than once; his right cheekbone shattered and healed into a crater. He is big and handsome and ravaged as a wrecked mill.

What would we have been doing, walking down the valley behind our father in convoy like this? Perhaps it was one of those Saturday mornings when he was off work. Then he would be taking us across to his sister's house, to Auntie Janet's, to play – though 'playing' at Auntie Janet's generally meant her getting me and Isobel to do her dusting or clean her windows for her, while Dad did odd jobs and then went off to get lunch from the butcher's, which sometimes saw him gone for hours.

He must have found it hard to fill those weekends with us, after our mother left. We lived with my nan on a small new estate built into the valleyside on the outskirts of Huddersfield. My mother was seventeen when I was born. My father and mother married quickly, in borrowed wedding clothes, when they knew I was on the way. He joined the force, then my mum moved into our nan's house in time for my arrival, and my sister was born the following year – just thirteen months between us. Christine, our nan, was the one who bathed and fed us. It was Nan who bought our school uniform each term and took us to the doctor's and went to our parents' evenings. It was Nan who ordered us to Sunday school, where we did colouring-in and learned about eternal hellfire. She was half-deaf from working in the mills as a child and everything she said to us she shouted. Have you fetched the milk in? Do you need your tea? Do you want your hair brushing? In Nan's house, reprimand and affection were indistinguishable.

Here we are, sitting together at her kitchen table: me, Isobel, Nan and Dad. Every evening, Nan would make us our supper and she'd ask my dad: *How was your day then, Pat?* She'd pour him tea and there'd always be buttered bread ready on the table. And sometimes Dad would say: *Not bad. Not bad. Mercifully quiet.* But other times his face would darken. Dad wasn't one for long stories, but he had a knack for disclosing the kinds of details that me and Isobel hoarded and picked over later, like magpies alighting on mysterious, darkly glittering objects. *Woman shows up at A&E*, my father says to our nan. *Tells them she doesn't know why her toddler won't stop crying. But the woman's covered in blood, and when they examine the poor kid, she's missing two of her toes. Woman was absolutely off her head. Pitiful it was. Absolutely pitiful.* Nan tuts. Then offers more bread and butter.

We learned in this way about cattle mutilation, and the specific injuries found on the bodies of children, and the ways in which

women could be drugged and hurt. We learned about the recklessness and violence of policemen too – *If I have to tell him again that
he's to lay off those girls . . . He did it in the back of the bloody van. They
think it's funny, these lads do, and the older ones aren't any better* – and
that if we were ever approached by a policeman, we were to immediately tell him Dad's name, rank and badge number. Not in order
to escape arrest: in order to protect ourselves from the officers.

I have only a small collection of memories of my mother and father
together, before Mum left, and in them my dad is boisterous.
Overbearing, even. He sweeps Isobel into the sky on Skegness
beach at Eastertime, a cuttingly cold blue day, and spins her round
as she screams and Mum shouts at him to stop. He holds my mum
tight in Nan's kitchen and sings into her neck, biting her shoulder
as she shrugs him away. We're at Hull Fair, where Isobel and I
each get to choose three rides, and Dad spoils us with toffees and
pop, and we see him kissing Mum when we're right at the top of
the roller coaster – is she trying to pull away from him? – then our
stomachs swoop as the carriage rushes us downwards.

When Isobel and I were young, our father would appear on the TV
every so often, and when he did, it meant that something terrible
had happened: an allegation against the police; a death in custody;
a riot. We knew that Dad appearing on the TV was a serious
business – and yet: There was Dad! On the TV! Had he had his
hair cut? He looked severe and handsome on screen. He scowled.
He used words we didn't understand. He wore his full uniform,
the peak of his hat shading his eyes as he stood, stiff, on the steps
of Huddersfield Police Station or the Magistrates' Court. Seeing
him made us giddy: we'd flit about the house after, waiting for him

to come home, asking him about lights and make-up, though he always just batted us away, retreating upstairs or straight out again.

His last TV appearance was after the Baby S case. He'd known, he said, that he'd be the fall guy as soon as they asked him to do the first TV interview. If there was something good on the horizon, the police authority spoke to reporters. But if something bad was coming down the line, if someone was going to need to take the rap, you might as well put them up in front of the cameras.

Watching him on screen was excruciating. There was a posture my father developed when he did the press conferences for that case. He was apologetic – at least his words were apologetic. He accepted that there had been grave failings; he extended his deepest sympathies to the wider family of the child. But he didn't look apologetic. His face, his shoulders, the tendons in his neck, his fists: they looked hard with fury.

Later, the details of various institutional failings would be released. In the Serious Case Review, the police were criticised for failing to share information; for failing to act on the information they received from neighbours, who had told them that the baby cried all hours of the day and night; for failing to act on information they received from a family member – an aunt who was worried when the baby and the mother hadn't been seen for weeks.

But before that, I had searched for the case at work. I wanted to see if the police had been mentioned in the judgment.

It was in that case report that I first read the list of injuries. That I first heard the rasp of a lighter.

It was in that case report that I discovered the work that could be done to a baby's body with just the tip of a cigarette. The ingenious harm that could be done by a father – and by a mother too.

*

What is my father like? He disappeared, after Baby S.

At my nan's funeral, the following year, he shakes people's hands, but he wears the same hardened look. Isobel sobs through the short service. *Hello, Dad*, she says, as we leave the crematorium. She's more submissive than I've ever known her; her words are a question. Dad turns away from her. She leaves then: *I can't stay, Grace – he won't even look at me.*

Later, at the end of the afternoon, when the sandwiches have been eaten and most people have gone home, I am washing up in Nan's old kitchen and I see Dad outside in the garden. He's leant up against a tree. He doubles over, vomits – once, twice – spits, then stands again.

Lillian is behind me: *He'll have had too much to drink*, she says. *That's all. Better not mention anything to him, love. He won't want you worrying.*

I don't mention it. Swallow it down. Eat your bread and butter, Grace.

We meet in pubs; in the desultory, dimly lit back rooms my father favours. I try to make conversation with him – though spending time alone as adults is a new facet of his early retirement, and we have no norms to default to.

One night, he gets the drinks in and then we sit down. He's hardly said a word. Bitter silent; unable to bear eye contact.

I default to work. I start to tell him about a big child sexual exploitation case in Rochdale – it's been in all the papers – and how I've been working through the court reports, and connections to Bradford and Huddersfield have come up. I think he might be interested in this but—

His heavy hands slam down hard on the table.

Fuck's sake, he says. *Do we have to talk about this?*

Then his head is in his hands.

Don't mind me, Grace, he says. *But let's talk about something else, eh?*

I rack my brains for something to talk about – anything other than work – and come up blank.

Every so often, when he's had a few to drink, he shatters his own silence: *I worked so hard*, he says to me one night, apropos of nothing. We're in the Black Horse again – a few months after his retirement – and he's downing the last of his pint. *When you and Isobel were small, I worked so bloody hard. And what good did it do. You never knew if you were going to make it worse by banging someone up or taking some kiddie away. I stopped wanting to intervene. So maybe it is my fault, maybe our lot ignored the information because they knew I'd be on them like a ton of bricks if they intervened too soon. That poor little lad. I'm paying for it now. God knows I'm paying for it now.*

We spend a quiet Christmas Day together. Ryan cooks a turkey with all the trimmings and his attentions to me are assiduous in the manner of someone who is channelling their terror into activity. Put your feet up, Grace. Do you want more gravy? What about cranberry sauce? More Christmas pudding? The way Ryan looks at me and my belly now: I sense the silent intake of breath each time.

And it isn't so different for me: when I catch a glimpse of myself in the mirror, the body that appears there is magnificently alien. I am aware, of course, that something is growing inside me – I can feel it nudging my internal organs every so often. But this most physical of experiences is still hard for me to conceptualise as the development of a baby. When I try to think about my body harbouring an actual infant, I feel light-headed.

I've done what's required of me: I've attended my appointments with the midwife and I've gone for blood tests and scans. I've memorised the list of toxins and harmful activities in pregnancy. I've been avoiding alcohol and soft cheeses and animal excrement and hot tubs and recreational drugs and hair dye and cigarettes and dry cleaners' shops, though I've read enough to know that you cannot keep a pregnancy properly clean and safe; flame retardant and DDT and forever chemicals find their way into placental tissue and foetal organs and breast milk whatever you do to try to avoid it.

What I haven't done is bought anything for the baby yet. We are waiting for the New Year sales, when there might be a bargain. That's when I'll find a way to prepare for the birth too. The baby is due in the third week of January, and I'll start my maternity leave a fortnight before that. I will have a week left at work after the Christmas break to sort things, then I'll do what I've always done: I'll cram. I'll use that fortnight to read all the books people have recommended to me. I'll perform whatever arcane activities are necessary to ready yourself for giving birth – practising yoga and buying essential oils and sitting majestically astride a birthing ball.

I nap often in those days between Christmas and New Year. I wake disoriented from long, repetitive dream sequences in which someone has given me a baby and I've lost it. It's somewhere around here, surely, I just put it down for a moment on this park bench, at the edge of this canal, next to this mine shaft, at this motorway intersection.

I take long baths. I take long, slow walks, which ease the sciatic tingle down the back of my left thigh. I show Ryan around the city and the Greenway – the cycle path that loops around the disused rail line. Ryan's starting to get his bearings. He goes out on independent missions and comes back with beers and takeaways. He's planning to buy a second-hand bike so he can get out more. He's identified someone at work who can score resin for him, so he might be able to sleep better. He says he likes York – that it's got loads of charm – but when he sits on the sofa next to me, he still rasps his thumb against the wheel of his lighter over and over, making a blister rise.

On New Year's Eve, I feel a surge of something. A subtle lift in my mood; a pleasure that pulses through me like the echo of an orgasm. I look out from the flat over the city walls – there are already small eruptions of light, fireworks being let off early. Maybe things will be OK. Pregnancies can turn out well. I have no risk factors. I have a job to return to and a willing partner. Maybe this eyes-squeezed-tight-shut joyride of a pregnancy will end with a lucky escape from disaster.

Ryan and I watch for the displays at midnight out of the bedroom window: rockets scream above us, accelerating into the dark, then falling back to earth in flurries of coloured fire. When they've burned away, they leave the sky hazed and sulphurous.

Ryan asks me, shyly, if he can sleep next to me tonight.

Yes, I say.

Ryan is careful: he curls his body around mine, the bones of his big knuckles resting on my hard stomach.

On New Year's Day, I walk into town to meet an old school friend. She has driven over from the valley. We buy tea from a kiosk and walk around the city – which is quiet now, the New Year's revellers drawn far off again, leaving behind a spill of shattered glass and chip trays.

Stacey married young – when we were just nineteen – and she has three children. I ask her what I should do to prepare for the birth.

Just take all the drugs, she says. Take everything you're offered. It fucking hurts.

I laugh, though she's not smiling. People's experience of birthing drugs seems to vary wildly. One woman at work told me that
pethidine, a commonly used painkiller in labour, is the worst – that
it made her sick and dissociated after the birth. But my boss told
me that pethidine was the absolute best thing about giving birth.
Get. The. Pethidine.

Between us, Stacey says to me, me and my sister have had eleven
pregnancies.

I can't make sense of this. Stacey has three children and her
sister has two. How do you get to eleven from that?

I had four miscarriages, Stacey says, between Jack and Millie,
and my sister had one miscarriage and a stillbirth.

I don't know what to say. I am sorry that I didn't know any this,
and that I didn't do anything to help. But I'm also affronted. Who
talks about excruciating pain and stillbirth to a heavily pregnant
woman?

The pains begin in the night. Except I don't think of them as pains. They begin so softly, so very gently, little nudges in my lower back reminding me that there is something that I need to do.

It is three weeks before my due date. It is the middle of the night. I try to go back to sleep, to get some rest, to fold myself back into the soft burrow of the bed.

Ryan has slept through his alarm. I can hear it going off in the living room. It's 2 January.

I shout through to remind him it's a work day.

He's in a rush then, trying to locate his things, cursing his way towards the door, when something in my face must stop him.

You OK? he asks.

Bad night, I say. I don't know. This aching in my back.

What should I do? he asks. I could call in?

Ryan doesn't qualify for paid paternity leave, but the café are going to let him take annual leave for a fortnight when the baby arrives. It's handy for them that it's January, their quietest time in the year. I don't want him wasting a day of his leave on a bit of sciatica.

No, I say. Go in to work. I'm going to the office. Just, maybe have your phone on if you can. I'll call you if anything changes.

The atmosphere in the office is gloomy. Nadine from the employment law team is up on a desk pulling down all the tinsel. Someone else says we should leave everything up until the sixth, but Nadine gives them a look: Come off it, she says. It's over.

Everyone looks exhausted. Except Tariq. He is close to ecstatic.

Whole day to myself, he says to me. A whole day without any crying or shitting or biting. And that's just the in-laws! I'm over the moon, mate.

He is like this all morning: insufferably chipper.

Things are quiet in the courts over Christmas. I work on the most urgent cases from late December. I am covering reports for someone who's still on leave, adding <*keywords*> in alphabetical order:

Conditions of detention
Inhuman or degrading treatment
Overcrowding
Prison conditions

The sensation builds in my body so gradually that I am able to ignore it for most of the morning. Every so often, there's a twinge deep in my back; it forces me up from my desk, to walk about to disperse it.

At lunchtime, Tariq and I head to the canteen together.

Just a sec, I say. I double over in the corridor, panting.

Right, that's it, Tariq says. We're shutting up shop. I'm calling you a cab.

No, it'll pass in a minute, I say. I just need to keep moving.

Grace, he says. Listen to yourself. *It'll pass in a minute.* What passes in a minute? A contraction, Grace, a contraction passes in a minute.

Tariq gets his phone out.

Look, he says to me. No one wants to see you birth a baby here. Do you think it's sanitary to deliver a baby under a colony of bats? Be clever about this and get yourself home. You can work from there if you really want to. But Grace, I think you're in labour.

I want my lunch first, I say. If this really is it, then I want to carbo-load for what's coming.

We sit in the canteen and I shovel-down macaroni cheese double-time while Tariq calls the taxi firm.

Back in the flat, I open up my laptop, log in to the remote system and begin to work on my cases again.

I add XML content tags. I skim the detail of the text for house style anomalies:

Increasing prison estates results in a rising prison population and a continuation of the cycle of imprisonment, degrading punishment and re-imprisonment.

Is there something off with the grammar of attribution here? Should I edit that out of passive voice?

When the pain comes, I snort at it.

My stomach flexes. The length of my bump hardens: it makes me think of an armadillo's back. I've read about Braxton Hicks, the way the body sometimes warms up for labour by practising contractions. I'd know if I were in labour. There would surely be some definitive sign; a transmogrification via which I will become *labouring woman*.

*

When Ryan arrives home after work, I am on all fours on the living-room floor, panting.

What the fuck, he says. Grace, why didn't you call?

It's nothing, I shout.

Right, he says, right, right, right. We need to time things. I'm setting my timer now.

He faffs about with his phone. He says a lot of *fuck*s.

It is three minutes between the pains. It is regularly three minutes between the pains.

We locate the plastic folder that the midwife gave me – I'm meant to keep it with me at all times, but I've hidden it from myself in a bedside drawer. I ring the number for the maternity ward and speak to a midwife who asks me what my pains feel like and how long they last and how often they are coming.

Don't come in yet, she says to me. I can tell from your voice that you're not close. You're too calm. Have a bath. Keep timing the contractions. Take some paracetamol.

Contractions. I want to laugh when she says that word.

When the pain returns, I'm down on my knees, groaning.

Two minutes, Ryan says. They're two minutes apart! I think we need to go now, Grace.

No, I say.

I go to the toilet. Nothing dramatic. No great release of waters. But when I stand back up, I feel something fall away from me. There, in the toilet bowl – a new, mysterious being; an intricate jellyfish, composed of blood and opaque tissue.

I expected water when I went into labour, lots of it gushing from me, not this strange gelatinous issue. I accept, then, that something totally alien is happening to me.

*

A taxi drives us to the maternity unit at speed. Ryan and the driver are silent as I bellow and my body bucks.

Good luck, the driver says, with evident relief, when he drops us at the door.

Inside the ward, we join a queue to speak to a midwife, and I begin to strip.

I'm not making decisions. My body is just happening like this.

I get on to my hands and knees in the corridor.

Ryan stares at me, stunned. I'm in my bra and jeans now. I regret putting on leopard-print underwear and heavy eyeliner this morning. I was going to buy birthing clothes when my leave started – clothes that were maternal looking, plain and soft, made from bamboo. I was planning to metamorphose into someone preternaturally composed, someone capable of birthing serenely, during my leave.

A woman helps me into a side room. It's a staff training room with no furniture, but there are padded mats on the floor, so I can kneel in more comfort and howl without upsetting the other women.

There's no space on the assessment ward, the woman says to us, but I don't think you need assessing, lovely. I think you're already starting to push.

The hospital is filling with a flurry of New Year babies. Later, I'll discover that other women who came to the ward that night were sent elsewhere – they were put into ambulances and taken to Scarborough and Leeds to deliver their babies. I am lucky to be given this side room, and then to be wheeled to a birthing room in my underwear, bellowing from the chair.

*

In the birthing room I beg the midwife, Becky, to get me into water.

I'll try, she says, I'll get the taps running, but it might be that we don't have time. I am already in *transition*, she says: the point where my contractions will hit their peak and I will be pushing hard and fast.

The water gushes. I push and I push but time has stopped. I am somewhere else, where the rain scores into the earth and the wind moans and the landscape is eternal.

Ryan helps me into the birthing pool. Then there is distant laughter – these two strangers, Becky and Ryan, chatting in the corner of the room.

I am far away from them. I am on the other side. Pushing. And the force of the push is the force of a building storm: the wind howling across the valley, flattening the heather, rushing up over Marsden Moor, tearing up trees by the roots, tunnelling all the way to Dovestones Edge and the Boggart Stones. Rain lashing the earth, water gushing rushing dragging broken spoils back down the valleysides – a tree trunk, a drowned sheep, great gluts of mud swept along by this force.

A woman's face looms in close to mine. Ryan says you'd like music, she says. Is that right, my love?

No words. I have *transitioned*. I am elemental now.

A small speaker starts playing Kate Bush. I must have mentioned this to Ryan, when I thought music would be useful. I had imagined that giving birth might be like the final hour on the dance floor and that the right tune would urge you on when your legs were about to give way.

The sound coming from the speakers is risibly thin.

No, I shout. At least, I think I shout it. Am I making any sound?

There's ringing in my ears. The aftermath of cacophony; of natural disaster.

I am pushing again. Though phrasing it like that makes it sound as though it is an effort or an act of my will on my part. I have no say in the matter.

I am nowhere in this push. And then I am everywhere: rushing up Scapegoat Hill, over Wessenden Reservoir, across the tops of the Pennines, to the terribly beautiful places, hearing myself howl through the wind.

The storm abates; releases me.

In the moment after that push, I see something in the water.

That's it, I think – that's the baby's head. I've done it.

When I look again, I see that it is only the plug in the tub below me, distorted under the water to look bigger than it is.

I could have cried then. Perhaps I do. Perhaps I am crying.

The midwife tries to give me gas and air, but I cannot make my breathing coincide with the pain. Instead, I bite down on the mouthpiece, and I wring Ryan's hand, and I cry out when my body contracts and the world accelerates through me again.

If I were to drown, I think, wordlessly, if I could just sink under this water and drown.

We've gotten stuck, haven't we? the midwife's voice says from the other side. You've been pushing for over three hours now, my love, and you're getting tired. I need you to move around.

I see a boy's face, and the fear that grips him. He's speaking to me, this desperate, handsome stranger, silently pleading with me. *My name's Ryan, by the way*, this boy once said to me, so very long ago.

I try to get on my knees. A birthing pool is not so much a pool as a large bath. It is hard to move around, it is hard to remember how my body works. I turn in the water, up on all fours, then the push sets in again.

There is no respite from it now.

That dark night wind scouring the valley bottom, rushing through the alleyways, wasteland, woodland, all the way up to the moortop. And that terrible moaning above the moors; from deep within the earth.

Two women enter the room. I see their mouths working, though I cannot hear their voices, there's just the ringing in my ears – and then their soundless shouting – their faces make two howling Os—

She's stuck, I hear. One woman's voice breaks through to me, insistent with fear. The cord's around her neck. We're going to need to pull her. Get ready.

Absolute tearing out. I am watching as they disinter my baby; as they drag my insides out between my legs: the wild, red, burning release of it.

My freshly filleted body flips over in the water; and then this raw scrap of life is bundled straight on to my chest – so big, so unbelievably big and boiling hot this lozenge of flesh.

Ryan-by-the-way is crying.

There now, there now, the midwife says to him. She's OK. She's breathing fine now. There we are.

Afterwards, they wrap me and the baby in towels and I sit on a special reclining chair with the baby hugged to my chest.

They give me an injection when the afterbirth does not come away. I refuse it at first. Surely the placenta will just be birthed of its own accord, when it's ready?

What a shame it would be, the consultant says to me, his voice wheedling as a threat, to have your baby here in this pool and then to need to go to surgery to remove your placenta.

The midwife speaks more gently to me after the consultant has left.

They're not really set up for natural afterbirths, she says. There isn't time. They'll give you an hour, and then you might end up with a C-section.

I accept the injection then; it makes me jittery and nauseated, as though I'm coming up from a pill.

And then I am pushing again, my body bracing, and the midwife tugs, keeps tugging, and the great bloody cord is drawn from inside me, keeps coming, dragging behind it this rich, black secret: the placenta.

I want to see it; this new and short-lived organ. The midwife arranges it on floor, on an absorbent pad.

It is unearthly beautiful. A complex gleaming thing. The veins branch like a tree; the exposed vessels are intricate as a naked lung. The dark red density of it, spread on the ground, is reminiscent of a heart, cross-sectioned: sliced in two, then pried right open.

Ryan asks me who he should call. My dad, my sister?

The world outside of this room is hard to fathom. Phantasmagoric, that place with taxis and money and fully clothed people.

I ask what time it is.

It's late, he says. Almost midnight.

Text them then, I say. And tell my sister to tell our mum. And message Tariq too. Tell him my maternity leave's started.

<warning – anomalous content>

The midwife ministers to me ever so tenderly. I am taken to a small room for my stitches. As she sews me back together, she tells me how careful she is being – that she practices needlecraft at home, that my tear is second-degree, which might sound bad, but it just means that a bit of the muscle has torn along with my skin. If only her shoulder hadn't gotten stuck, the midwife says. It was going so well. But we had to do that little tug at the end, didn't we?

I learned the word 'episiotomy' just a few weeks ago. Meaning: an incision to the vulva to assist with birth. A woman at work told me not to let them cut me. She said that 'natural tearing' was now best practice, and preferable to cutting. She'd been cut, when she had her second baby, and she wished she'd been allowed to *tear naturally*. That had sounded to me like the most horrible of oxymorons. I didn't want to be having this conversation in the shared kitchen at work in the three minutes before my next meeting with a woman I now disliked. Who on earth could happily commit to the prospect of one's own intimate tearing as *natural*?

But now it has happened, I am ascendant. Yes, I have been torn apart, in the most tender place, and here I still am. Alive.

Alive. Alive is the beat of my heart, and the pulse of the blood still coming away from me, and the beat of my baby's heart too.

The midwife runs a bath for me and makes me toast, which I cannot eat. I am too jittery with aliveness. I lie back in the hospital bath and survey the water: my blood runs through it in rich streams. My body has survived and it is magnificent – torn and spasming and loose and exhausted as it is. I am submerged in the deep water of living. Waves of euphoria from sheer *being*. I have never been cared for like this before. A man called Ryan – a lad, truth be told – holds my baby, holds my baby right against the skin of his chest as I sink into this hot bath. Alive. My baby. Weird incantations beating in my mind.

Women of various ages and backgrounds weave around me and the baby to take care of us. Becky is soon gone, and an older woman wheels me to the maternity ward. She suggests that Ryan head back to the flat to get some sleep. This woman will be there all through the night if I need her, she tells me. It is this woman who finds my baby some clothes and shows me how to change a nappy, with a gentle tutting when I tell her that I have brought no hospital bag or nappies or baby clothes with me. And this woman then places the baby back on my chest, adjusts her position, and watches as I try to feed her.

Yes, yes, that's it, just like that, you're doing it, my love.

The baby's latch is amazingly fierce and biting for such a small creature, and it makes me gasp – my uterus flinching along with each movement of the baby's mouth.

Is it meant to hurt like this? I ask.

That's a good sign, the midwife says. It means your uterus is contracting again, getting smaller now baby's here. Feeding helps to speed things up. You'll only be producing colostrum just now, not milk. That's the golden stuff. Every ounce counts. Look at her working away, getting every last drop.

When I place the baby into her little box – a plastic case next to my hospital bed – I cannot sleep. But the baby sleeps. In a too-big navy babygrow, in a little hat knitted by a stranger, under a boil-washed blanket, in that box next to me. The hospital feels warm and subterranean, and there is no one else on the ward through most of the night. I watch the baby, my baby, folded deep into her own being; I listen to the midwives moving along the corridors, greeting each other, assembling for periodic cups of tea, rushing to where they are needed. I hear cries from other women, at the dark peak of their own labours. The distant background hum of life going on, of routineness, while I lie back on the hospital bed, almost swooning with the wonder of my life still gushing through me and out of me and pulsing through this dark little organ next to me. My own small movements – tentative steps to the bathroom, which bring fresh blood, the rearrangement of the baby's blanket – are muffled and sacred.

My gratitude is off the fucking scale.

Later, people will ask me about the birth. Friends and doctors and alternative therapists whom I'll consult in the hope of making sense of what is happening to me. It isn't necessarily that they want the gory details. But they expect the disclosure of trauma. They expect the experience of the birth to explain the state that I am in. Their heads incline and their voices drop. And how *was* the birth? they'll ask me.

But the birth was not at all screaming humiliating haemorrhaging splitting shitting terror.

My baby's birth is a shimmering blood-bright out-of-time event.

What was happening, what had happened to my body, seemed impossible. And yet, it was absolutely happening. I had survived the crash. My baby had survived too. We had pushed through together, tearing into the warmth and squall of new life.

It is hard to tell what time it is in the hospital. The ward's rhythms are not properly diurnal. The lights are dim, but people come periodically to my bedside to check the baby over. Someone tests the baby's hearing. Someone else arrives to check that the baby has filled a nappy. A smartly dressed woman comes to me with a folder full of information and promotional vouchers for nappies and formula and tries to talk me into a baby photo shoot. Someone else comes to check the baby's reflexes and that she can grip. Can that be right? That seems to be what this bedside visitor is saying to me.

The baby is small, at the cusp of being premature, but she has been quick to latch and, as she has passed these various tests, I am told that I am allowed to take her home. It is the morning after the birth. The lights on the ward are brighter now and Ryan is back with us. A new midwife is telling me this, nonchalantly: You can go home now, if you like.

I want to say to her: But I've only just arrived!

Instead, I nod. This new midwife is not unkind, but she speaks to me with indifference: my going home is no skin off her nose. *If you like.* The baby weighs 2.63 kilograms, or five pounds thirteen ounces, and she is at the eighth percentile for weight – the fiftieth percentile being the average. This is not good news, obviously, the midwife says to me and Ryan, but someone's got to be in the low percentiles, and just as long as baby keeps feeding, you're not to worry. Just feed the baby, the midwife tells me, just keep feeding the baby. That's all you need to do. That's your job now. It's that simple. Another midwife will come and visit you at home in a few days' time and she'll weigh the baby and help if there are any problems.

But the first problem is the pram: in that, we don't have one. We leave the hospital with the raw baby bundled up in blankets in Ryan's arms. The walk is short, but I have to take it very slowly – prolapse is a risk after birth, and the midwife has cautioned me against walking too far. When we step outside, the baby's face is exposed to the drizzle and it hurts to see that. I take her from Ryan and try to shield her. But I feel unsteady, as though my legs might give way, so I hand her back. Prams, I now realise, are armoured vehicles for babies; they're the shell around the naked clam.

When we arrive back at the flat, Ryan and I turn towards each other in the hallway: *What do we do now?* Neither of us moves – we scent the vapours of each other's fear. Something rises in my throat, like a laugh, but more uncertain. Ryan breaks away, busying himself arranging a blanket on the living-room carpet, telling me he needs to go into town to get nappies and clothes and a cot.

When he's gone, I place the baby down on the floor and watch her flinching there. She looks catastrophically small on the carpet. When she cries, it is a quiet, broken sound. I want to pick her up and hold her close – right against my heart – but that desire feels so intense that it alarms me. I hold myself back. I don't know how much I am allowed to pick the baby up and hold her. How much is too much?

Ryan comes home with newborn babygrows – which are all too big – and size-zero nappies and a Moses basket. We search online and order a sling and a pram, and I join baby groups on Facebook and google everything that I should have found out already. I do my cramming belatedly, in a sleep-deprived frenzy. Search terms: *Where should your baby sleep / How much should a baby sleep / How often should a baby feed / What are the best positions for breastfeeding / How often should you hold a baby.*

The baby feeds and feeds in those first few days. She bleats whenever I put her down. We watch tutorials on how to change a nappy and we learn about the different stages of baby faeces: the thick, tar-like meconium that comes first, flushing out everything the baby has ingested in the womb; then the mustard-coloured, scentless milk waste that follows. Ryan changes the baby and makes me cups of tea, and I sit on the sofa feeding her and asking the internet questions. The hours disappear like this.

We make lists of possible names and stick them on post-its around the flat: Sylvia. Nancy. Courtney. Florence. Chrissy. Violet. None of these words fits our raw, wordless scrap of baby.

The baby yawns for the first time and her eyes dilate on contact with light. Her irises are a fickle metallic colour that is difficult to decipher. Olive. Amber. Pewter. The baby feeds. The baby feeds some more. I try out different positions, nesting on the sofa with cushions all around me.

I read about the fourth trimester: the idea that newborn babies need to remain cocooned by the caregiver's body even after birth.

Newborn babies are softer and rawer than any other newborn mammal. A human baby needs a caregiver's body continually close to protect it, to pattern their breathing and to regulate their temperature. The baby needs my heartbeat to develop the rhythm of her own.

My breasts are swelling with milk. They throb whenever the baby cries. My heart throbs too. I am euphoric still: we have made it through. We have made it through to the other side of birth – which is surely life. I have survived with only a tear and delivered this warm-blooded organ into my own arms.

That first night at home together, we set up the Moses basket next to my bed. We lay the baby down to sleep with great ceremony, but of course the baby will not sleep there. She wants my body. The nightlight is a small crescent of brightness in the dark blur of milk and skin and adrenaline that the night becomes. The baby makes such noises, such terrible tiny rasps and rattles and sighs, as though breathing is altogether too difficult – as though she might give it up on the turn of each breath. Half-blind, she gasps all night long, searching for me with her mouth, searching for me with her tiny broken cry, never settling out of my arms.

Ryan sleeps through most of this. I listen all through the quiet hours to the baby's bizarre, guttural sounds. In the middle of that first night at home, I watch the baby repeatedly flinch herself awake in the basket. I check on her breathing again and again.

And the baby doesn't look like something new in the darkness then.

The baby looks like something ancient and broken. An injured relic. Dark-sea fish, dredged from the Midnight Zone, sputtering up water. Cawing pterodactyl of an infant.

I think there must be something wrong.

Or, I don't think it: I feel it. In those darkest hours just before dawn, the night begins to hum around me. I taste metal in my mouth.

But when morning comes, Ryan googles and tells me that the sounds the baby makes are totally normal. All newborn babies make such noises. She's clearing her lungs of amniotic fluid, he says: she's becoming a land mammal.

We call our baby Rosa – her skin is mottled like crushed petals – and we register her birth at the office in town.

In the first week after Rosa's birth, things arrive in the post each morning. Cards and flowers and little knitted hats from people I haven't seen for years and from Ryan's friends and family whom I've never met. From my mother: a tiny cardigan, wrapped in tissue paper, with butterfly buttons. The cardigan is implausibly, comedically small, but is still too big. I message my mother to thank her, and I send her a picture of Rosa, but I receive no reply.

On our second evening at home, Eileen, an older woman who lives down the corridor, knocks quietly on our door. She has brought a cake, warm from the oven, wrapped in tinfoil, which she hands over to me. The cake feels significantly more substantial than my infant.

If there's anything you need, Eileen says, whispering, anything at all, you just let me know.

Do you want to see the baby? I ask.

Oh, I don't want to intrude, Eileen says.

Come in, I say, opening the door wide, please come in.

We sit on the sofa, and I hold Rosa towards the woman.

Eileen coos and says she is lovely, but she does not attempt to hold her.

I'll leave you to it, she says after only a few minutes, still whispering, and gets up to leave.

At the door, I have to check a sudden impulse to catch hold of Eileen, to beg her to stay, come back inside, *please*, please stay with me and my baby.

My milk is coming in. My breasts keep on swelling until they are hard and painful and overflow the baby's latch. Rosa feeds and feeds and feeds and cries if I put her down.

A new midwife comes to visit us and weighs the baby using a steel scale. It looks like a piece of equipment from a butcher's shop. I have to lay Rosa on to this cold metal plate. She is naked and screaming.

The midwife tells us we are doing great. *Fantastic, in fact!* The baby has lost no weight, which is excellent – usually they lose in the first few days before the mother's milk comes in properly. And with a baby this small, there could be problems with feeding. But the baby is feeding ferociously, prodigiously. The baby is a feeding machine. *Just keep doing what you're doing!*

My father and Lillian come to visit, bringing biscuits and flowers. Lillian fusses over Rosa in whispers, but the baby just wants to feed. Lillian kisses her on her little hatted head. My father sits on the sofa, impassive. He looks out of the window; he looks into the distance beyond the car park. He looks as though he's waiting for a jury verdict to come in. Lillian does the washing-up for me, and then they leave.

*

Here we are then, me and Ryan-by-the-way, together in the darkest fold of January, alone with our baby. The pram arrives. Ryan
brings it up in the lift and fettles it. We are going to take the baby
for a walk. We attempt to wrap her in a new pram suit, but the
suit is too big and too stiff. The baby's limbs are hunched up, frog-
like, and cannot be made to straighten into the arms. Who knew
that babies were so ill-fitted to clothing? We give up and lay the
baby down on the suit instead, wrapping the sleeves around her,
putting on her hat, covering her with three blankets. Rosa endures
the bundling up. She is quiet as we wheel her out into the dark and
the cold, as we jostle for priority: Let me push. No, let me! This is
only the baby's second-ever walk out into the world. Her first-ever
experience of sleet. It is the point in a Yorkshire winter when the
sky never seems to get properly light. The Christmas decorations
are still strung in bare trees and above the shops. Windows glow
in the dusk and, once we are on the main road, the world moves
away from us – separating into different distances. Being inside
the flat has warped my perception of depth: the close-upness of
it, the close-upness of the baby. But here, just at this moment, the
street lamps are coming on, one after the other, down the avenue
that leads towards the Minster, the future glimmering ahead of us.

I'm usually good at relating to people. Even the most difficult and unpredictable ones – that is, everyone in my family.

For instance: I am with my nan after school, as we watch TV together in her living room. When an advert for sanitary products comes on, Nan hisses at the screen, hitting the mute button. *Mucky bitch*, she says, though the advert only shows a woman turning her face to the sun in an open-top car. *Mucky bitch* is also what Nan calls our next-door neighbour, Jill, on account of her once having sunbathed topless in her own back yard.

I learn when to stay quiet through my nan's tirades, and I learn when she might allow me to chide her.

Nan, I'll say, when I'm older and braver. What's mucky about some blue dye on a sanitary towel?

We didn't used to *hang everything out*, she says. We didn't have to *parade ourselves* like that. Everyone's got to show everything off these days. Your Auntie Elsie had a prolapse after her fourth baby, and she didn't even see a doctor about it. You remember? She just took care of it herself, popped it back inside when it bothered her.

And did it end well for Auntie Elsie? I ask, knowing my nan's sister died of a haemorrhage.

Well, it doesn't *end* well for anyone, does it? Nan says, pleased with herself.

For instance: I am on a night out with Isobel. We've gone across to Leeds together, to a club night at the Dark Arches, where we dance on cobblestones in the network of vaults under the railway station. We queue for the Portaloos with girls whose faces glow with the internal heat of Ecstasy, who talk to us like long-lost friends. *I'm getting tired*, I tell Isobel, late into the night. *I'm not going to stay out for much longer. I've got a big week at work ahead.* Isobel is pissed off about this. She really needs a decent night out, she tells me. The music doesn't stop until 5 a.m. and we've paid for the full night and we've hardly gotten going. She goes to buy us more drinks. Later – who knows how much later – I'm jittery as fuck, needing to dance, needing to move, needing to talk, then needing to vomit. *I think I've been spiked*, I say to Isobel. *I'm sweating and I don't know what to do with myself. Did you leave our drinks anywhere? But why would anyone spike a drink with something that brings you up like this?* She confesses to me, then. She spiked my drink with methamphetamine. *It's just to give you a little boost, Gracie. Don't be angry. I just want you to enjoy yourself!*

There are plenty of other times that Isobel has put me in danger: Isobel shoplifts when stressed and has been known to slip her stash into my bag in the big M&S in Leeds. Isobel once hid my passport so I couldn't go away to Ibiza without her. I always, eventually, forgive Isobel, and find a way to understand her.

For instance: I'll hear nothing from my mother for weeks on end, and then I'll receive a long text in the middle of the night. Sometimes she attaches pictures of old photographs she keeps in an album at her house of me and Isobel from the 1980s, with our matching pageboy haircuts and highly flammable shell suits. When I reply and suggest that we might try to meet up, she'll go quiet again. My mother's patterns of contact are intermittent at best, but I know that she gives what she can, and that what she gives is painful for her. My mother left when I was nine years old. I have accommodated her absence; I've tried to understand and empathise, and I usually succeed.

Given all this, it should be easy, surely, to relate to my own infant. I didn't spend much time around babies before Rosa was born, but people look after babies every day, without any special training or qualification. *This is your job now*, the midwife had told me. And I've always been good at my job. I am reading the literature now, exhaustedly swotting up on baby care, learning all the lingo and the parenting philosophies – the fourth trimester, the first 1,000 days, feeding on demand, attachment parenting.

Yet the baby is not relatable.

The baby is not even recognisably human.

She still rasps and wheezes through the night, like an infant reptile. Like a prehistoric creature fighting to survive.

When she needs to feed, she noses blindly, like a newborn terrier or ferret.

The back of her body is all bone, her little shoulder blades like vestigial wings.

She has small tufts of hair on her ears, which are pointed and battish.

The stump of umbilical remained part of her belly for days before it turned black and splintered away, like rotten tree bark.

The soft spot on Rosa's head is the most alien thing of all: the skull not yet fully formed, the bone softening at the top into I don't know what. Tissue? Organ? Brain? Covered with only the thinnest veneer of skin. Rosa's soft spot pulses in and out with her heartbeat. It looks alive. It's awful-raw-throb.

The baby is not at all relatable.

The truth is, she frightens me.

And yet, I am consumed by caring for this weird little lozenge of almost-life. Unprecedented, alien, rawness of the baby. My baby. Broken-bird, pulsing-brain, internal-organ of a love object.

It is hard to keep track of the days; and of whether it's dusk or the diminished light of a midwinter morning. I have not slept for more than a few minutes at a time since Rosa's birth. At night, she still flinches herself awake, issuing her weird, broken sounds. When she's quiet, I check again and again that she is breathing.

Sometimes in the mornings, Ryan takes her into the living room, telling me I should rest. He likes to hold Rosa in the crook of his arm while he makes toast, speaking to her in a low, adoring voice. I can't sleep even when he takes her. When Rosa is out of my sight, my heart quickens; when I hear her cry in the next room, I can taste metal in my mouth. And Ryan isn't careful enough with the baby. He swings her around on his forearm and enjoys the challenge of boiling a kettle while he balances her there. I have to steel myself to let him hold her or take her out of my sight.

What day is it? What time is it? Day five. Ryan tells me it is day five after Rosa's birth, and this means we need to return to the hospital for the Heel Prick Test. The baby's heel must be punctured and her blood drawn in this arcane medical ritual. There are so many tests that are administered on a newborn – so many things that can go awry.

*

It is, at first, comforting to be back at the hospital. The low, dim corridors and the full-on heating: it's like being folded back into a maternal warren. On that first night when we stayed here, I hadn't even known how to change a nappy! And that kind stranger, the midwife whose name I'll never know, showed me, patiently, in the small, quiet hours, how to clean the baby, how to feed her and hold her, though that midwife must have had a hundred other urgent things to attend to.

When my name is called, we wheel the pram into a small room, where a nurse is waiting for us.

Right, we need to get baby undressed, the nurse says. So I can get to baby's heel.

We entered the realm of no definite articles when Rosa was born. *We're just going to check baby over / We just need to see if baby responds / And has mum been to the loo yet? / And would dad like to hold baby?* Medical professionals refer to us as archetypes. I need a moment to process the grammar of these new requests.

I do not find it easy to undress baby. Rosa's limbs seem entirely unfit for clothing, and her body is so fragile that I fear pulling or pushing too hard. When I lie Rosa down on the medical couch and begin to undo the poppers of her suit, she starts to cry.

It takes me over when she cries like this. My body flinches; the milk in my breasts flinches.

Oh, poor thing, the nurse says, then laughs. You were so warm and snug, weren't you?

The nurse approaches Rosa with a needle. This smiling stranger is about to pierce my baby's foot and take her blood.

When it happens, the blood is shockingly red: a small, bright bead on the baby's heel.

Five quick pricks of the needle, a circle of blood to keep the baby safe.

The baby's cry is ringing through the air, my breasts throbbing with each wail.

Oh, says the nurse, sorry, it's taking a little while to clot there.

I need to get the baby dressed. I need to put the baby to my breast. While the blood is still beading, I jimmy Rosa's legs back into her babygrow.

That might stain a bit, the nurse says. There's no need to rush.

But I do need to rush. I am all rush. Rosa's little mouth is working to find me; her cry will break me apart.

My milk is really coming in now. Those first few days after the birth – when I was just making rich, fatty colostrum – were nothing compared to this. Now, when Rosa feeds, it feels as though my breasts are bursting into her mouth. My bump has almost entirely disappeared. Everything is changing so quickly, my body surging with the baby's needs, swelling and shrinking with tidal force.

I need to feed the baby. I need to get home and feed the baby.

We walk as quickly as we can, Rosa mewling in the pram the whole way round the ring road. By the time we reach the entrance to our block of flats, I am wild with my need to feed her.

I scoop Rosa out of the pram and tell Ryan we will take the stairs. The lift is all the way up on the top floor and, even though it will probably be quicker, I can't wait.

The staircase in our block of flats is a wide spiral and I bundle Rosa in close, pushing my lips against her warm head as I start to climb, building to an almost-run. When I reach our floor, the fifth floor, I glance down through the open stairwell. The tiled hallway is a long way below us and the distance makes me woozy. The ground floor seems to accelerate away from us.

I watch Rosa spill from my arms.

I watch her tip over the banister and fall all the way down through the stairwell.

I hear the sick sound of overripe fruit splitting against a hard surface.

My stomach swoops. The air is ringing. The taste of metal floods my mouth.

Rosa is still here against my chest, wailing and pulsing at my throat.

I hold her even tighter and run inside.

Ryan is already in the hallway with the pram. I do not stop to take off my coat. I go straight to the sofa and pull at my clothes until I unlatch my bra and Rosa's mouth finds what it needs.

When I feed Rosa, I experience a moment of swoony relief – and then waves of panic, coming on like contractions.

The air around me is still singing with danger. My thoughts are tumbling.

I saw Rosa falling through the stairwell.

I heard Rosa hitting the floor. That awful wet thud.

I know then – deep in my gut, in the ringing through my skull – that my baby is not safe with me.

The air sang to me like this long ago. I am awake at the dead of night in the bedroom I used to share with Isobel, in our nan's old house. I am nine years old. My mother has left, we don't know where to, and I am sleepless, wondering where she might be – is she close by, hidden from us in this valley, or far off, somewhere unknown? Total darkness. Everyone else is sleeping. But the house is not silent, far from it. Ripping through the night is the great roar of an engine. More than one. Joyriders. Lads from town steal cars and drive them out here at night, as fast as they can, racing along the valley bottom and up the road by our estate – the road out of Huddersfield towards Saddleworth. They race up the valley and then total the cars at the top, leaving them burnt out on the moor. The sound of the revving is enormous. It's as though the valley is being torn open. Long after the engines have died away, I'm left with an echo ringing in the air and though I try to sleep, I can't. I see the valley around me in the darkness, alive with danger. I travel to all the forbidden places in my mind: to the Titanic – the empty, black mill in the valley bottom below us; to the lonely, winding paths next to the canal and the blind alleys that run behind the old coal yards and the pubs; to Scapegoat Hill and Marsden Moor, and up, up over Saddleworth Moor to the most desolate of places – to Dovestones Edge and the Boggart Stones, where children lie, moaning with the wind, under the gorse and the heather.

I try to blink away the vision of Rosa falling from my arms. I press my palms against my eye sockets. But the vision is persistent. It shows up again behind my retina as an after-image.

I can't eat the dinner Ryan has cooked for us.

What's up? Ryan asks. You don't like it?

I don't feel right, I say.

Oh, he says. Can I get you anything? Hope you're not coming down with something.

I see Rosa slip down through the stairwell. I hear the awful sound.

At Rosa's bath-time, I find the sight of her nakedness close to unbearable. Her raw sweet smell. The vulnerability of her tiny limbs.

I ask Ryan if he'll put her in her sleepsuit. I watch as he tries to get her limbs to comply. Don't press down on her belly like that, I say, as he tries to hold her fast while he does the poppers. You'll hurt her.

I make a rule:

I will not use the stairs again. I will never take the stairs again.

There: a problem, and a solution.

But I cannot sleep that night, not even the brief grey blur of rest I have become accustomed to.

When I close my eyes, I see my baby fall; I hear her body split against the tiles.

A health visitor comes to see us. She looks around the flat suspiciously and runs through questions on her clipboard. Do we smoke? Ryan stares at his hands. She marks a cross on the sheet. The health visitor has the demeanour of a parental probation officer, checking our risk factors for offending. Do we ingest drugs? Are there any problems with anger in our relationship? The health visitor asks to see where the baby sleeps. And you're breastfeeding? she asks me. Do you bring her into the bed with you when you feed her? Whatever you do, don't fall asleep while you're feeding her in bed or on the sofa. Babies get crushed that way.

We return to the living room and she runs through a list of further dangers, regaling me with stories of infants who have died in mind-boggling circumstances: toddlers who crashed into unsecured flat-screen TVs, who became tangled in the cords of window blinds (the health visitor looks around the flat at this point, to check for such cords); infants who swallowed watch batteries and tiny screws. A child in the US suffocated when a bottle of baby powder was inexpertly opened and its contents filled the air. A toddler in the UK died after ingesting a toilet cleansing block.

She leaves us with a leaflet about *Safety in the Home*. It includes

a to-do list, and each instruction conjures the ghost of a serious
case of harm:

> *Check that your medication and cleaning products are stored securely.*
> *Put child locks on all low cupboards and drawers.*
> *Always fill your child's bath with cold water first and then add*
> *the hot.*
> *Keep chargers out of reach and unplugged when not in use.*
> *Remain with your child in the kitchen at all times.*
> *Ensure you have working smoke alarms and carbon monoxide*
> *detectors.*
> *Keep nappy stacks out of reach to avoid suffocation.*
> *Make sure your baby sleeps in a separate bed near to you.*
> *Ensure that your baby sleeps away from radiators.*
> *Ensure that your baby's bed is free of choke hazards.*
> *Ensure that you stay with your baby even during daytime naps.*
> *Don't ever leave your baby on a bed, sofa or other raised surface.*
> *Install a fireguard.*
> *Keep your windows locked.*
> *Keep cigarettes and lighters out of reach.*

I hear the rasp of that lighter. The fizz of a burn into soft flesh.

There are, apparently, countless ways in which an infant can
expire. But I already know this. I feel how fragile my baby's life is
in every interaction with her, every time I gather Rosa up, every
stutter of her breath.

I remove all the blankets from Rosa's bed. I watch her as she
sleeps. I handle her with demented reverence, afraid that I will
fall, that I will drop her. Because I knew before the health visitor
came: my baby is not safe.

Ryan's family arrive in convoy. The first to come are his father, Alan, and his father's girlfriend, Charlie. Alan and Charlie sit together on the sofa while I feed Rosa. They look at each other to avoid looking at the point where Rosa's mouth meets my breast. When Alan addresses a question to me, he answers it himself – *Of course she won't be sleeping well. They never do at this stage* – as though feeding the baby renders me mute.

Alan and Charlie have booked into a hotel for the night and are planning to go out for the evening in York. They are both dressed in ironed white shirts and tight jeans. They have a reservation at a steak house and Alan checks his watch every few minutes. He is only a decade older than me; Charlie is closer to Ryan's age than mine.

Ryan makes us all tea, then he loiters next to me, waiting to hand the baby over to his father. He places his hand on my shoulder, then removes it. I know that his relationship with his father is uneasy; that after his parents divorced, his elder brother went with his father, and Ryan stayed with his mother. Ryan sits on a kitchen chair and starts to play with his lighter. Rasp, rasp. I will Rosa to finish feeding of her own accord, so that I don't have to try to extricate my fountainous nipple from her mouth in front of everyone. So that she won't bleat with abjection when she first meets her grandfather.

We wait and wait. Then the baby lets my nipple go.

Ryan lifts Rosa over to his father, who bundles her up close.

What a bobby-dazzler, Alan says.

When Charlie holds the baby, she puts her nose to Rosa's head.

Aw, she says, she's beautiful. Watch out, Alan, she says. This is making me well broody.

Nah, Alan says. I've done my time at the messy end of babies. And you know how quickly they get bigger and turn into right ugly little bastards, like our Ryan.

Fuck's sake, Ryan says, under his breath.

Never could take a joke, Alan says. Take a photo of us then.

The picture on Ryan's phone is of Alan and Charlie grinning above Rosa, while she sleeps, secretive as a larva, in Alan's arms.

Ryan's mother, Paula, visits a few days later. She cries when she sees the baby.

Oh, she says, oh, it just brings it all back. They get big so quickly. You won't believe how quickly. This is the best time. Come on, come to Granny.

Paula doesn't want to let go of the baby. Not even when the baby is crying for milk.

Let me try to settle her, Paula says. I'm a dab hand. And you must be exhausted. Ryan says you're not sleeping. Why don't I take her out for a bit in the pram and try to settle her that way? If you feed her all the time she'll only come to expect it. I had my boys on a two-hour routine from the get-go and it worked a treat. Feed, play, sleep. Feed, play, sleep. Never feed to sleep. You'll make a rod for your own back. If you express for the night-times, then Ryan can feed her. And I can come across and stay sometimes to give you both a break. Shhhh, baby, shhhh, no need for all this fuss.

The baby's mouth is a bright red alarm call. My heart is beating through the milk in my chest; it's beating hard through my nipples.

Thanks, I say to Paula, but I think I just need to feed her now, if you don't mind.

Paula bristles around the flat after that. She motions to Ryan to huddle with her in the hallway, where I can't hear what they're saying.

Ryan comes back in looking sheepish.

Mum wants to look around town, he says, at the big M&S. Would you be OK if we popped out for a bit, like an hour max? I've told her that you need to feed Rosa and we never know how long that will take, so . . .

He mouths silently at me: *You OK?*

I nod.

Ryan's older brother, Luke, and his girlfriend, Chloe, arrive next. They bring pink gift bags full of pink clothing and pink headbands. They show no desire to hold Rosa, which is initially a relief. Luke seems restless and scans the flat, as though looking for escape routes. Chloe talks about the best time in the year to have a baby, and how September babies are the smartest, and summer babies are the most artistic. She tells me that the optimum gap before you have a sibling is probably three years. She says that her sister is four years older than her, and that worked well too. She says you have to think about these things, don't you, when you have a baby, because only children are usually messed up. She has a friend who's an only child and she has serious problems. Like, *really serious*. And if you have a boy and it's an only child, that's a big suicide risk, isn't it? With girls you have to worry about different things. Like eating disorders. And friendship groups. And anyone can get into drugs if they go to the wrong school, can't they?

Wow, Chloe says, there's so much to think about, isn't there?

Each of these visits is wearing. It is unnerving to think that the baby, my baby, who feels so much like an organ of mine, is related to these hard white strangers with their erratic modes of communication. That these people have a claim to the baby now.

But I also find that as each visit is coming to an end, I don't want Ryan's family to leave. I want to maul Charlie's clean white shirt and pull her back inside the flat. I want to lay my head on Chloe's shoulder and weep into her straightened, fragrant hair as she intones about cyber-bullying and pornography and body dysmorphia. I want to make things OK with Paula and ask her to feed the baby in the night: *Yes, please, take her away from me, show me how to do it, show me the magic of the two-hour routine.* An unfamiliar ache when Paula leaves: *Come back, Paula. Come back and show me what it's like to be mothered.*

All through these visits I harbour the secret of what I have seen.

Ryan's annual leave has vaporised in this weird fortnight after Rosa's birth – a long, blue, pre-dawn blur. On his last day of leave, we decide to go into town to get coffee at a fancy deli and this is how I plan to manage it:

I will not take the stairs with the baby.

I will not go near any stairs with the baby.

The morning is cold and sharply beautiful: bright blue skies, the peregrine falcons screeching above the Minster. Rosa has fed for hours, we have changed her nappy, and the plan is that we will walk and she will fall asleep.

But Rosa is not sleeping. She is squalling in her pram as we enter the city centre and when we reach the café, there's a long queue outside.

Fuck's sake, says Ryan.

Rosa's cry hitches up a notch.

I can't come in with her wailing like this, I say to Ryan. I'll try walking her for a few minutes longer while you queue. Maybe get a takeaway if she doesn't settle?

I push the pram towards Lendal Bridge. Rosa's cry is so unremitting that I can't work out how she's still breathing. Do infants have circular breath, like yodellers, or is she going to hyperventilate? My breasts are throbbing. I need to feed her.

Midway across the bridge I glance down at the river surging under us. The cold, deep gush of it.

I stop dead.

I watch myself unzip the cover of the pram as Rosa continues to scream.

I am lifting Rosa out of her pram. I am offering my baby, with trembling hands, to the river.

The sound of Rosa hitting the water. The sensation of total coldness overwhelming her. The water closing over her.

A heat haze shimmers across the bridge ahead of me, though the day is perishing cold.

Rosa is still safe in her pram. In fact, she has stopped crying.

I begin to run. I need to keep moving; if I don't let go of the pram, if I don't look at the water, then what I have seen can never happen.

I run to the other side of the bridge, and then I walk, as fast as I can, away from the river, gripping the pram handle so tight that my knuckles are white.

I saw a woman enter the river from Lendal Bridge once. At least, I saw the aftermath. I had been walking across the bridge with Tariq when suddenly everything seemed to go quiet. I didn't hear the body hitting the water: it was more like an absence of sound, a collective intake of breath. Pedestrians on the bridge froze, staring down at the river. Someone from below, someone working on one of the river cruise boats moored there, started shouting.

Here, here, he was shouting, and he stood at the side of the boat and moved a pole through the water. But there was nothing to see: only the calm, dark, reflective surface of the Ouse.

People on the bridge were using their phones, taking photographs. A few minutes later, the police arrived and blocked the road and made the pedestrians disperse.

Tariq and I didn't speak to each other, but both us were drawn to stay. We walked in synchrony down the steps to the riverside and stayed there as search teams arrived on small speedboats and circled the legs of the bridge, moving progressively further downstream. A helicopter honed in above us and hovered in the air before following the course of the river. Back up on the bridge, paramedics arrived alongside the police and two divers began to kit up: it was a bitterly cold day, I remember that, and I had thought then about what it would be like to enter the freezing water. To plunge right into it with barely a splash. To become river.

A man walked past me and Tariq, and said to us, leering: *What are you waiting for? It's a body they're looking for now, you know. You waiting to see a body?*

We stood for a few minutes longer and then moved off, returning to whatever it was that the day ahead held for us.

I had seen a headline, weeks later. The body of the woman had been discovered near the village of Cawood, ten miles downstream.

Ryan is calling – has already called several times – and now I answer.

I tell him we're at Micklegate Bar, past the train station, and to come and find us. Please.

I pace with the pram up and down the street. If I can just keep away from the water—

A story comes back to me, a story by Annie Proulx that I read long ago at university. 'People in Hell Just Want a Drink of Water'. I re-enter the world of that story as you would enter a river: I am totally submersed. It begins with the landscape. I am in the Wyoming *wild country*. The shadows of clouds make me queasy; their mottled shapes over the rocks. The air hisses in this place. *It is like a deep note that cannot be heard but is felt, it is like a claw in the gut.* On this land, every kind of tragedy has occurred – misadventure, slaughter, cruelty. But earth and sky persist. The story narrates the horrible fate of Ras, a young man catastrophically injured in a car accident, though the character who returns to me most forcefully now is Ras's mother. She is a sensitive woman – visited by *nerves* and *fretted by shrill sounds* – who wrote poetry as a child. She gives birth to a baby girl who cries *intolerably*. The family make a journey by wagon across the Little Laramie River, and the woman stands up in the wagon, suddenly: then she hurls her crying baby into the water. *The child's white dress filled with air and it floated a few yards in the swift current, then disappeared.* The woman shrieks, tries to leap into the river after her baby, is held back by the men. The men gallop the horses down the river's edge. But the baby is gone.

Afterwards, the woman ties her remaining children to chairs in the kitchen, to try to keep them safe from harm. In the night, she checks on them in their beds repeatedly, *to learn if they had smothered.*

I am that woman. I am Ras's mother with *her nerves*, acting in a *fit of destruction*. You could just do that, your own hands throwing your own baby into the water, irrevocably.

A lad on the street is saying something to me. He's looking at me with worry; he touches my arm.

Ryan. Ryan repeating his question: Are you OK?

Please, I say, will you push Rosa home?

York is a city of floods. Every year since I've moved here, the river has flooded. I've stood on Lendal Bridge and looked out over a flood plain. One surprising thing about flood water is that, despite its violence, it often looks entirely still: the water makes its own damage disappear under the surface. But if you look closer, there are always clues to its force. Once, I saw a bare tree caught up under a bridge, which might have been swept all the way from the moortops. Another time, I saw a dead sheep tangled amongst the ropes of the cruise boats. The Aire, the Wharfe, the Swale and the Nidd all converge in the River Ouse. The rain that falls on the Pennines, the rain that falls in the Dales and the North Yorkshire Moors, pours down into the Ouse. Days after downpours in distant Yorkshire valleys, the Ouse will flood.

In good weather, the river looks even more sedate. In the city centre, pubs and bars extend outwards from older buildings to create terraces over the water, and these terraces fill up with drinkers each weekend – drinkers who every so often, on particularly warm summer's evenings, will ignore the signs at the edge of the water and jump right in. The river is deceptive. The currents are always strong. Every year, the Ouse swallows a portion of the drunk and the desperate who enter it.

The city of York has two rivers. The Ouse is the river that everyone expects. York is built around the Ouse: it flows between the train station and the Minster, and you must cross it to enter the city from the west. There are nine bridges across the Ouse, Ouse Bridge being the oldest, connecting the rest of the city to Micklegate, the only steep hill in York, at the top of which is a medieval gated entrance. Scarborough Railway Bridge came next, built in the 1800s, when York railway station was the largest in the world. The newest bridge is the Millennium Bridge. It crosses the Ouse a little way out of the city centre, where the river passes the university campus and splits fields to flow out towards Selby and Goole, all the way to the Humber Estuary. Coney Street, the main shopping street in York, backs right on to the Ouse; the great old buildings of York – the print works and the Mansion House of the Lord Mayor and the timber merchants – descend right into the water. On winter nights, the banks of the river here look more like Amsterdam or Ghent than a northern English city.

The other river, the river that visitors are less likely to anticipate or come to visit, is the Foss. The Foss rises out in the Howardian Hills, and then snakes its way south and around the city, until it merges with the Ouse at the Blue Bridge. There are sixteen small bridges and passageways that cross this river. People sit alongside the Foss by the ring road to drink the day away; swans nest here and children walk the riverside paths. Near to my block of flats, the Foss curves under willow trees and ash, and folk gather here to inhale nitrous oxide or to fish with magnets for scrap metal. In spring, hawthorn blossom crowds the riverbanks. In autumn, blackberries grow fat here.

And all of this is to say: it's very difficult to move around York without crossing a river. It is hard to plot a route further than about half a mile from my flat, for instance, and even that distance requires careful planning. But this is what I begin to do. I will not take the stairs with the baby. I will not cross a bridge with the baby. And then, perhaps, Rosa will be safe.

It is my first full day alone with Rosa. Ryan has gone back to work, and I have ten hours ahead of me.

I am going to meet my father and Lillian in a café. I check the map on my phone to navigate a route into town that avoids crossing a river. I have chosen a café that I know can be reached by such a route, but I check again.

I settle Rosa into her pram, and as I do this, I stop myself looking out of the windows of our flat, at the bare branches of the lime tree, because a new awareness of our height above the car park has begun to make me feel queasy.

In the corridor, I do not let myself look at the stairwell as I walk to the lift.

Then, once I'm outside, I turn straight up Monkgate. I will not let allow myself even a glance towards the River Foss, which winds behind me.

My father and Lillian are inside already. It is tricky to steer the pram over the step at the threshold to the café and then between the closely packed tables. Rosa is wrapped up against the cold, but the café is warm, so now I need to take off her pram suit and layers of clothes.

My father and Lillian watch me wrestle for a while then Lillian offers to hold Rosa while I try to undress her.

I hesitate. Lillian has held babies before. Lillian had twins, for Christ's sake.

I lift Rosa over to Lillian, but then she starts to cry.

Oh, Lillian says, do you need your mummy? Do you need your mummy?

Lillian rocks Rosa back and forth as she says this.

The baby wails.

I can taste Lillian's perfume from across the table. It's so strong, it must be an assault to Rosa's delicate nasal passages.

She might want feeding, I say to Lillian. I'll take her.

You'll spoil her, Lillian says.

Ha, I say, though I can't tell if Lillian is joking.

We pass Rosa between us as though manoeuvring an unex-ploded bomb.

I need to feed Rosa in a way that isn't going to be horrifying for all involved, so I reach for the 'feeding apron', which I bought late one night when it showed up on my timeline. It has a strap that hooks around your neck, and then it's supposed to hang over you and shield the baby and your breast from public sight. I attempt to get it in place, one-handed, while Rosa screams. Then I attempt to unlatch my bra, but I can't do it while holding the baby safely and keeping the apron in position, and I am pretty sure that I've just flashed the couple on the table next to us. My breasts are throbbing with Rosa's screams. I can't get her in the right position, and I can't see what's going on under there.

Fuck this, I say. I pull the apron to one side, so that I can see Rosa and make sure I'm supporting her head properly.

Lillian and my dad look at each other and then down at the table. Then my dad positions his menu so that my breast is redacted from his sightline.

The baby is feeding ferociously, and my let-down is ferocious too – milk streaming down the baby's chin. I try to get comfy, but the café chairs have no arms, so I have to hold her in place using both of mine.

Lillian pushes a menu towards me.

The hotpot looks good, she says. Doesn't it, Patrick? What do you fancy, Grace?

I'm not sure, I say. Something I can eat one-handed. A cheese toastie?

Right, I'll go and order then, my dad says. My treat.

While he's up at the counter, Lillian leans in towards me. Her perfume truly is weapons-grade. I try to angle Rosa further away from her.

Are you doing OK, love? It's a big thing, your first day alone with a baby.

I want to say that I am doing OK. I am nodding to try to make that true. But I find that I am also crying. I don't want Lillian to see me crying but I can't even press my hands to my eyes, because I am holding the baby.

Oh, love, Lillian says. Oh, dear, dear. Don't cry, love. You've got a lovely healthy baby here. You've got nothing to cry about! You don't want your dad to see you like this, do you? He'll only worry. Let's get you cleaned up.

Lillian takes a napkin and smears it across my face.

When my father returns, Lillian is reminiscing about her twins, a boy and girl from her previous marriage who are now in their early twenties. Because she has twins, Lillian views parents of singletons with envy and condescension. All through my pregnancy, her favourite thing to say to me was: Now, imagine that *doubled*!

That first day I was home alone with the twins, Lillian is saying, we didn't even get out of the house. Not even close! If I wasn't changing or feeding one of them it was the other. And then they start crawling and you've never a moment to yourself. If I could have only had one, we'd have been all over the place, out and about. You've got to remember, my pram was twice that size. I couldn't even get it on the bus. Imagine that, but double!

Our drinks arrive: coffee for my father and Lillian, and a pot of tea for me. Only now I realise that I can't even pour my own tea.

Dad asks if I've heard from my mother or – he pauses – my sister.

Mum and Isobel are dangerous territory with Dad. If I tell him they haven't visited yet, he'll be angry; if I tell him they've been attentive, he'll be cynical about their motives.

I've had messages from them, I say. Mum sent a card and a little cardigan for Rosa. Isobel is going to come across to meet her soon, I think.

Right, my dad says, and his expression hardens. So they haven't been across yet? This movement in my father's face; it's the same stiffening sorrow of that final press conference. *I accept there have been institutional failings, and I extend my deepest sympathies.* He balls his fists on the tabletop.

I shouldn't expect much from your mother, he says. She'll find it hard. She could barely hold you or your sister, even when you were tiny. Your nan did all of that for her. And me, through the nights, when I could, I did it too.

I'll play mother, Lillian says, as she pours my tea. She hums a tune while she does this, then she places the metal teapot back on the table.

It sits there, inches from my baby's naked head as she feeds. My dad could knock the teapot over if he starts going off. If he starts listing my mother's weaknesses and sweeping his heavy fists around.

Or I could spill my own cup of tea.

My hand, lifting the water over Rosa, scalding tea spilling over her – over her soft face as she latches at my breast.

I watch her features dissolve into raw tissue.

My breath is ragged. My stomach roils.

But Rosa is still here, safe in my arms. Rosa still has an epidermis and eyes and lips.

My sandwich arrives, but I can't eat it. What the fuck is going on now. I'm menaced by a fucking pot of tea.

Lillian is talking again, but I'm not listening to what she's saying. I'm remembering a boy at my secondary school who'd suffered burns as a toddler. He'd pulled a pan of boiling water down over himself from a kitchen stove. His face and neck were sinew, even a decade later. That boy, Steve Murgatroyd, was bright and happy and brilliant at maths. He wanted to be a surgeon, and maybe he is a surgeon now. He was very brave, everyone agreed. You could see how close he'd come to not surviving every time you looked at him: every time he smiled, you could see the mechanics of his skull, and the veil of life was drawn right back.

I try not to look at that teapot. I concentrate on the tablecloth. And then I do something weird. I start counting.

If that girl over there makes it to the door by the time I count to three, then Rosa will be safe.

If those three people come into the café by the time I count to three, then things will be OK.

If that girl makes the coffee in three, two, one, then Rosa will never, ever be scalded with boiling water.

If you follow the rules, you'll stay safe. Are you listening to me, Grace? Stick to the main road. Stay in the playground. Be home before it's dark. Don't ever leave your sister. And don't you dare go anywhere near that mill that canal those woods Scapegoat Hill those moortops.

I am taking my sister to school and our nan, Christine, stands at the front door behind us, shouting in solicitous fury: Take care of our Isobel! Watch yourselves! Be home by dusk! The journey to school is fraught with danger. Firstly, there's the steep walk from our estate to the valley bottom. The quickest way down is to follow the ginnels that zigzag between blocks of flats and round the backs of pubs and houses, but we are forbidden from taking this route. Our nan has warned us that men stalk alleyways, waiting to expose themselves to young girls. We know that older kids gather to sniff glue by the bins behind the Black Horse, and that the skag-heads leave their needles there too. Our cousin, Billie, has shown us a stash of pornography he has discovered in the bushes by the snicket closest to our house – he takes us on a secret mission to see the cache, leafing through the crimped pages of one magazine, flaring female genitalia at us. We know we must avoid these ginnels and snickets, so I lead Isobel down the main road towards school, which brings its own risks. Speeding traffic. Boys who shout at us from cars. Older men who leer and sometimes veer towards us. Even the pathway between the main road and the school field requires careful navigation. There's broken glass. The school fence, scrawled with obscene graffiti – atavistic cocks and messages telling us what happens to snitches – nettles and long grass gobbed with cuckoo spit, which also looks obscene to me.

At school, the children around us have their own preoccupations, like Tamagotchi and Tetris and football cards and competitive violence. Isobel and I nurture our own obsession together. We create a constellation of fears to worship. In our bunk beds each night, we pass information to one other. We fill in the gaps in those stories that we hear from our father at teatime, the stories about cattle mutilation, and injuries found on the bodies of children, and the ways in which women can be hurt, and about the recklessness of policemen too. Isobel and I speak in whispers between our bunk beds about burns and abrasions and internal bleeding. We speculate on how much pain it might be possible for a body to feel before it expires. We alight on the most horrible details, a pair of magpies picking over our glittering treasure. Neither of us speaks directly about our mother, but her absence fuels our imaginations. She could be hidden in any of those places where we are forbidden to go: Titanic Mills, the car parks and ginnels that run behind old coal yards and pubs, the secluded crescents of greenspace next to the canal where people dump chest freezers that could easily accommodate a body.

In the daytime, we follow our nan's rules. We stick to the main roads. We arrive home before dusk. We don't talk to strangers. We don't go up Scapegoat Hill or to any of the forbidden places.

We mind the cracks and say Amen after the school prayer. But at night, when the air rings, the valley is alive around us, baroque with threat – the alleyways, wasteland, woodland, canal paths, Saddleworth Moor, Dovestones Edge, the Boggart Stones – all the terribly beautiful places, where the wind moans and the earth keeps its dark secrets. We cling to the rules, in the daytime: but no rules can stop the dark energy of this valley filling our dreams at night.

When Ryan gets back from work, it's already midnight dark and I've changed Rosa into her sleepsuit. I don't know why baby clothes are designed for day or night, why they're sold as playsuits or sleepsuits. It's all the same soft fabric for the baby to lie in, whether it's got moons and stars or rainbows on it. Perhaps it's to try to forge a connection back to the old diurnal patterns of life for the carer – a night-time when you could rest; a daytime that was bright and purposeful.

Ryan rushes into the living room, kisses me on the head, scoops up Rosa.

Oh, man, I've missed you both so much, he says.

Ryan is a visitor from another dimension. The cloth of his apron is cold and stiff; he smells of cigarettes and synthetic flavourings and other adult humans.

How has it been, he asks me, flying solo?

I don't know how to account for my day. I spent the whole afternoon feeding Rosa. When I tried to get up to make myself a drink, she screamed, and then she fell asleep in my arms, and I knew that if I moved at all she would wake – so I sat there, my shoulders aching, my phone tantalisingly out of reach, willing myself not to fall asleep for I don't know how long. The walls of the flat, the thick carpets, sometimes seem to inch towards me when I'm stuck like this; a weird visual effect of exhaustion.

I managed to get to that café to see my dad and Lillian, I say to Ryan. So that's something.

Great, he says. Nice one. What shall we have for dinner? I'm famished.

Dinner? I say. I don't know.

Oh, Ryan says, I didn't mean that you *should* have made it or anything. It's just been a long shift, and I've been prepping food and drinks all day so ... Maybe we should get takeout?

Maybe we should. Except my maternity pay only lasts for six weeks at the full rate, and Ryan is on minimum wage, and the baby's pram (which is *actually*, Ryan informed me, imitating the saleswoman, part of a *travel system* that comes with different fittings to adapt and grow with the baby), set me back the best part of eight hundred pounds. Ryan has no savings. In London, he lived hand to mouth from gigs and bar work, whatever presented itself. Sometimes he'd have a decent run of corporates and generous tips. There was one weekend when he took me out for champagne and oysters. And there'd been other weekends when I visited and he had nothing to eat on the boat but digestives and tinned tuna. Now he's on a static wage and no one really tips a barista.

Rosa starts to cry in Ryan's arms.

Is he holding her right? Did he wash his hands when he came in?

I can feel my pulse in my milk, in my throat, rising to meet Rosa's cry.

I'll take her, I say. Do whatever. Order a takeout. My card's in my purse.

*

Our new night-time routine when Ryan comes back from work: tea together, the baby's bath-time, and then we settle down to bed early. I sit propped up by pillows in bed and feed Rosa. *Whatever you do, don't fall asleep.* Ryan downloads a film or a series, but I can't watch TV now; even the low levels of peril being generated in the early stages of a drama make me nauseated with dread.

Ryan takes Rosa for a nappy change before lights-out, and then we try to settle her in her bed – her Moses basket, set up next to me, nested in the wooden rocking stand it came with. Ryan sleeps. Rosa flinches and frets and grizzles herself awake. Sometimes, I stay in bed and rock her with my foot. But when I do this, the basket gradually moves further and further away from me, until I can no longer reach it. The moment it stops moving, Rosa wakes and I start the process all over again.

I wish, then, that I was brave enough to take Rosa into the living room, or to walk her up and down in the pram in the hallway. But I am not. The hall has begun to narrow around me whenever I walk it with Rosa, tunnelling me towards the communal corridor and the staircase. And then I am walking with Rosa in a dream, I am walking with Rosa into a nightmare, I am holding her over the stairs again, letting her go into total silence.

So I avoid the hallway. I leave the bedroom as little as possible in the night, which means that I am stuck in this dark room for hours trying to soothe the baby to sleep. *Whatever you do, don't fall asleep while feeding the baby.*

Sometimes, when I am doing this, I think of the other women in the city around me, awake in the night too, broken by tiredness and solitude. Often, in the middle of those long winter nights, I think of the hospital. In fact, I long for it. The hospital is less than a mile away. I think of its warm, safe, windowless corridors.

I imagine the women travelling through them now. I long to go back to that first night after Rosa's birth, to that first night when we'd made it through – when I thought that we'd made it through. When I lay in that hot bath and surveyed it and saw that my body had survived. My blood ran through the water in rich streams. We had pushed through together, me and my baby, we had burst into the warmth and squall and blood of life. The background hum of the midwives about their business. My own movements around the baby – tucking her in, watching her sleep – muffled and sacred on that first night.

I long for the nocturnal company of the hospital, for the cast of midwives. To be close to those who are birthing and bleeding, who are rejoicing and grieving, to hear the cries of other women, at the dark peaks of their own labours.

Motherless. I catch my breath. Deep sudden sharp pain of it.

O f all those fears that we nurtured together, Isobel and I, our dearest was that something would happen to our mother. Our mother's movements were difficult to track at the best of times. Mum worked a succession of jobs with erratic hours – at the café at the leisure centre in town, which made her hair smell of chips; catering silver service at a hotel which kept her out late at night – but every so often, she'd be at the school gates to meet us with a plan for the afternoon. *Let's have an adventure*, she says, taking our hands. We travel into town on the bus, to a fairground that's landed outside the station. She buys us crisps and pop and fusses over us: *Are you too cold? Do you need a wee? Are you hungry? Are you getting tired?* When we get home, Nan is waiting for the three of us, tutting as though we've absconded. *You'll be wanting something proper to eat by this time, I should think.* Mum shrinks in front of Christine. She won't eat at the table with us. *Sorry. I should have thought. I'm sorry, girls. Your nan has something proper for you. No, I won't eat, Christine. I'd better be getting ready for work.*

I worry that Christine's glare will make our mother disappear entirely. I fear that Mum, who often comes home in the middle of the night, will be mown down by joyriders. I have dreams about Mum falling down manholes. The news is full of stories of contaminated meat and cannibalistic cows and I worry that Mum, who often prepares hamburgers at the leisure centre, already has BSE and is going to become totally deranged. My mother sometimes cries in her bedroom for what seems like days on end, and my father tells my nan that she is *losing the bloody plot*. I fear then that Mum might be locked up in Storthes Hall – the old mental hospital that looms at the edge of town – and that she'll become one of those blanched women people claim to see, silently screaming, in the windows there.

When Mum actually leaves, it takes several days for me and Isobel to notice. One day, after school, I clock that Mum's bedroom door is half-open – exactly as it had been that morning. I peer into the room. No trace of the vanilla scent she wears: no sign of her body under the duvet. I can't remember when I last saw her.

I don't think Mum slept here last night, I say to Isobel.

We decide to check on Mum's things. We look in the bathroom cabinet: the bag with Mum's lipsticks and powder compacts has gone. We check again in her bedroom: no sign of her nightclothes, which she usually leaves scrunched up in the bed. We check the hallway: her good boots and her work shoes are gone.

Isobel starts to cry. Christine discovers us in a state of panic in the hallway and I pluck up the courage to ask: *Where's Mum?* Though I want to say: *What have you done to her? What have you done with her?* We know all about *domestics*. We know that husbands finish off their wives on the regular; he just *turned*. What if Dad's done something to her? Christine might even have helped.

Nan does a lot of shushing and makes us sit down at the table for tea as usual. Isobel sobs as she stuffs fingers of bread and butter into her mouth.

Eventually, Christine says to us: *Your mother's ... not well. She's gone ... to try to get herself right again. Your father was going to tell you about it, but he's been on lates.*

I don't believe Christine. Not at first. The Moors Murderers worked together to bury the children who haunt the moortops above us. Men and women could work together, then, to dispatch women and children. What if my nan and dad have dispatched Mum together, and what if they decide to smother me and Isobel in the night?

When Isobel and I are sent to bed, I feel sick with fear and the air around me rings.

A letter arrives for me and Isobel. The postmark says Halifax and I recognise my mother's handwriting. We have not seen her for more than a month by now. She is unwell, the letter says. And she misses us very much. She misses us every day. But we will be better off with our nan and our dad until she gets better.

There are visits with our mother. We are taken to a pub in town by our nan. Mum cries when we first walk in and then she keeps disappearing into the loos. She hugs us too tight; she begins to shake and cry as she breathes into our hair. When Nan says it's time for us to be getting home, Isobel starts to cry too. *When are you coming home? When are you coming home? It's Christmas soon. And then it'll be my birthday. Will you be home by then?* I sense that asking this question makes it less and less likely that Mum will ever reappear, so I shush Isobel and tell Mum it's OK; we are both OK. I don't tell her that Isobel has started wetting the bed and that I'm up at all hours listening to joyriders and wondering if

Dad will snuff us out in our beds. We're OK, Mum, I say. We'll see you soon.

Mum never does come home.

M orning half-light. Rosa crying and Ryan already gone to work. Rosa wants to feed, but however much I feed her, it doesn't seem to work. That is: she only wants more and more. More milk, more of me. I have no way of knowing how long each feeding session will last – it could be ten minutes or half an hour or a two-hour stretch. Her hunger is like a sinkhole, widening by the day.

Sometimes, after a long feed, I try to stand, and there is nothing left. I can't *even*. She is sucking the marrow from my bones. One time, she feeds for over an hour, and then she's sick and most of the milk spills back over me and the sofa. I cry, soundless, at the sheer waste and at the pitifulness of not even managing to brush my own teeth that morning.

Rosa stares at me intently as her mouth works to make my milk come faster. And her eyes are magnetising. They're changing – darkening in colour, but also seeming to shimmer like amber. I know, now, how much a baby's eyes alter – not only that the shade of a newborn's iris changes with time, but that a baby's vision changes rapidly too. A newborn cannot see far, not much beyond the distance from a parent's arms to their face. Colours are only distinguished later in the infant's first year. A newborn's eyes cannot track movement or depth. The caregiver's face is the entire visual field of the baby.

Sometimes, Rosa focuses on my face with such ardency it unnerves me: her silent gaze makes me think of locked-in syndrome.

My own vision has altered since the birth. I am meant to be showing Rosa the world, but my own visual field is shrinking to the dimensions of the flat, the walls and plush carpet that thickens around me. Details of Rosa's body fill the screen in close up. The circles of cradle cap that form, lichen-like, across her scalp. A hangnail the size of a half-grain of rice. The pulse of her soft spot.

Looking at the baby has become reciprocal myopia.

Sometimes, I put her down in her basket and turn to do something else – go to the toilet or stack the dishwasher – and when I turn back to her, I experience an acute visual shock. The baby is tiny. The baby is an absolute jot! The world outside the window, the lime tree and the supermarket car park and the ring road and the city beyond, speed away from me then, in a rush of depth and distance. And this sudden smallness of the baby is just as unnerving as her enlargement.

It is a kind of rapture, to hold Rosa close this morning. The smell of her scalp, which is warm and yeasty – a mix of fresh baked bread and semen. The dimpled flesh of her thighs. The tufts of hair on her ears. The soft new fat at her neck. The intricacy of her hands and feet, just beginning to articulate themselves. The smell of her breath – like clotted cream left out of the fridge.

And God, how I love Rosa's tongue. Sometimes, she sucks her own top lip and makes a frill of it, and it looks like the polyped skirt of an aquatic creature. Every so often, her tongue flickers outwards, as though she is tasting the air. She scallops her tongue, making it palpitate when she wants the milk to come faster and when she does this, I feel the palpitation through my whole body. My breasts throb with milk. And I feel the palpitation in my own tongue too – a sympathetic pulse, an echo of my own infant feeding. Rosa's tongue throbs through all the most tender places.

I wonder, in a moment of rapture, holding Rosa, why people ever saw fit to create the idea of a soul, when the body is so holy.

And then I realise, in a flood of terror: because the body is so brief. Because the body can be marred in a moment.

These are the things I have to get rid of:

The tin-opener, with its serrated wheel glinting on the kitchen worktop.

The matches by the microwave.

The screwdriver under the sink.

The plastic packaging from the baby mattress that Ryan stashed in the hallway, ignoring the printed WARNING: *To avoid the risk of suffocation keep this bag away from babies and children.*

While Rosa sleeps, I stalk around the flat, looking for dangerous objects.

I put the kitchen knives and scissors into a special drawer, and (new rule) I won't let myself open this drawer.

There is a blunt razor that has lived on the side of my bath for so long that its slats have grown green. I bin it.

As I clear these objects away, I count. I spin the ring on my left hand – my nan's old ring, passed on to me because of her arthritic knuckles long before she died. I am trying to spin the ring in a full circle with each count, to make the tiny glitter of a diamond line up back where it began, on the count of three. If it does, if it lines up perfectly, then maybe things will be OK.

Rosa will never be harmed by a screwdriver matches tin-opener polythene scissors.

Ryan has a stash of lighters in his bedside drawer. As I open the drawer, I hear the rasp of flame, licking blue against soft, sweet baby flesh.

Into the bin. One two three.

I scour cupboards for batteries and bin them too.

I pour all our bleach products down the drain.

I hide Ryan's good watch – I know that it harbours a tiny, lethal battery inside its belly.

I disappear things into bin bags and dump them out in the hallway.

I want to get rid of more. I want to get rid of every electrical appliance in the flat and pull the gas pipes out by the root.

But there's no way to complete this process, because practically any object could be fatal for an infant. A coin. A kirby grip. A biro. For Christ's sake, you could probably finish off an infant with dental floss if you put your mind to it. And my mind does go to it. I am the warder of my own prison. Everything inside the flat has become contraband. A paperweight. A cocktail stick. I could probably do the baby in with a teaspoon.

When Ryan arrives home that evening, he looks around with suspicion.

I tell him that I've had a tidy-up. I got rid of all that plastic in the hall, I say. That's what's in the bin bags.

Later, he says: This is going to sound weird, Grace, but I thought I bought loo cleaner the other day. And I can't find my watch. I'm pretty sure it was on the bedside table. Any chance you know where it is?

I had hoped that the chaos of new things in the flat, the piles of tiny vests, the stacks of nappies and blankets and swaddle cloths, would cover for me for longer.

It'll be here somewhere, I say. I'll keep an eye out.

Later still, I hear Ryan whispering to his mum on the phone: I think so, Mum. I guess she's just tired. That's normal, right? But . . . I don't know. Stuff keeps moving around and disappearing. Like, the cutlery. And now I can't find my watch. She's hardly sleeping. I'm not sure. I just feel a bit . . . clueless.

Tasks that would once have seemed small, such as writing a thank-you note or going to a shop or to the post office, now require significant planning and the navigation of new rules. But I have to get outside of the flat and its ever-thickening walls, so I try to set myself small activities for each day. For instance: I need to go to the Children's Centre to have Rosa weighed.

As I walk, I count and I look for good omens. If I see two magpies or I count the right number for something – the speed with which I manage to cross a road, the number of cars to turn a corner before the lights change – then there is momentary relief. Things might be OK. Rosa might be safe.

When I reach a road bridge, I grip the pram tightly. The wind is high and it tunnels through the grey sky, and I feel the world speed up around me, a whoosh of vertigo.

Moving as quickly as I can, I start to cross, counting as I go, not letting my hands move from the pram handle. Perhaps, from the outside, I look like a mother lost in the rapture of my baby.

Hey! Grace! Hey!

A woman stands in front of me, blocking my path.

Grace! she says.

It's Lucy from the office, with her big headphones and her glittery lipstick and her morning hangover, whom I have sat next to almost every working day for the last six years, whose habits and diurnal rhythms I used to know intimately, whom I last saw six weeks ago – in another lifetime.

Sorry, I say. I didn't see you there.

What are you doing out here at commuting time? Lucy says. Let's see this baby then. She peers into the pram. Aw, she's so tiny. Everyone in the office is dying to see her. How come you haven't sent a picture?

Oh, I say. I didn't think to. Honestly, I'm so tired I don't know what I'm doing.

My sister had a really hard time when our little Jack was born, Lucy says. She said to me she only survived it by telling herself, over and over, every day: I will never have to do this again. I will never have to do this again. And then she got pregnant with Millie and she was over the moon. What I'm saying is, I think it gets better. But then, what do I know?

I'd better get off, I say. We're on our way to the Children's Centre. Having a newborn is a bit like looking after a prize pig, or a boxer, you know. All of these weigh-ins you have to attend.

Right, says Lucy. Well, don't be a stranger. We miss you. The system crashed the week after you went on leave and we couldn't upload anything for a full twenty-four hours. Tariq almost had a stroke. We've had a whip-round for some vouchers. John Lewis. Tariq's going to bring them across to you. He'll be well jel that I got to see the baby first. Take care, Grace.

Lucy leans in to hug me. Her hair smells of raspberry

conditioner and the freedom to have a shower and I want to stay with her, to follow her all the way to work, to sit at my desk and apply my mind to organising all the content in my cases, to hierarchise the information, to apply house style rules, to tag something all the way to perfection.

The waiting area at the Children's Centre is a chaos of women and babies and prams and pacifiers and change bags and teething toys. One by one, we are invited into the small room that is occupied by the midwife.

Now then, my love, she says to me when it's our turn, I'm going to need you to take baby's clothes off for the weigh-in.

I am embarrassed, again, by my own ineptness at undressing my baby. When I've stripped her down to her nappy, the midwife says: You'll need to take that off too. We need a true weight.

When Rosa is totally naked, she trembles, her skin purpling with the cold almost instantly. She begins to mewl. At home, I keep Rosa clothed as much as possible. Seeing her raw skin makes me giddy with fear.

Aw, says the midwife, laughing. I know, I know. Poor little thing. It'll all be over soon.

My body is starting to throb.

The midwife puts a blue paper towel over the cold metal surface of the weighing scale and asks me to place the baby on it. The midwife clucks at Rosa and strokes her cheek as she presses a unit measurement button; she works cheerfully, as though there is no urgency whatsoever.

I can hardly bear it – Rosa squalling like that and her nakedness. I scan the midwife's room for dangerous objects, which are everywhere. Steel scissors, steel needles, the heavy block of the weighing scales itself, which if dropped on to the baby would smash—

Oh, she's doing well, the midwife is saying. Tenth percentile now, and she started off so small, eighth percentile I think, wasn't it? Well done, mum. Keep it up, keep the feeding up, and she'll keep her weight up. She's thriving.

Thriving. What a wild idea when she's in so much danger.

Right, the midwife says. Let's get baby dressed, shall we?

I put Rosa on the floor to dress her. The sight of my naked baby on the linoleum is appalling. I struggle to find a nappy in the change bag, then I struggle to put it on.

Let me, the midwife says. I know how many times a day you have to do this.

She lifts Rosa by her legs and has her in a nappy and then back in her suit in almost no time.

I didn't know you were allowed to do that – just lift the baby like that. In the nappy tutorials I've watched, the paediatrician says that lifting a baby up by the legs could compress its spine and cause damage. The softness of the newborn's spine is why they shouldn't travel for long in car seats either. The internet has taught me that a baby's body is softer and rawer at birth than any other mammal's, that a newborn needs a caregiver's constant vigilance, she needs a caregiver's body continually close, to pattern her own breathing; to regulate her temperature; even to develop the rhythm of her own heartbeat. The internet has not taught me how to bear being responsible for another creature's heartbeat.

Rosa is screaming.

Is it OK, I say, if I feed her? And perhaps I say it so dejectedly that I trigger the midwife's concern, because she says: Of course, you don't need to ask. I'm going to write in your red book to record baby's weight and I'm going to get you a glass of water and then let's have a little chat about *you*.

And how *was* the birth? the midwife asks me, with her head inclined. And how are you feeling *in yourself*? Has anyone talked to you about postnatal depression? she asks. Have you ever experienced depression before, my love?

No, I say.

Are you sleeping? she asks.

Not really, I say. The baby only goes to sleep when she's feeding, and I know you can't fall asleep with the baby, I know how dangerous it is, so I stay awake—

Well, the midwife cuts me off. There's the official guidance on that, which I can't speak against. But what I can tell you is that if you're breastfeeding and not consuming alcohol or drugs, many women do find that it's necessary to bed share and there are ways to make it as safe as possible.

The midwife writes me a list of the names of support groups in the area and where they meet – a breastfeeding support group in the Groves; a coffee morning at the Children's Centre; a baby yoga class in Bishopthorpe.

She asks about a support network. Do I have one? But who has a support network at 4 a.m. on a Thursday morning?

And dad, says the midwife. Is he around?

The baby's father, the midwife means, not my own: we are back in the realm of the archetype.

I tell her that he's around, though he works quite long shifts just now.

They're long days and nights, aren't they, especially with the dark in the winter. Try to get out each day, if you can. You're lucky, the midwife says, that your milk's coming in so strong. For lots of people, if they get stressed, the milk stops. Do you think you might be able to go and speak to your doctor, to get a check-up? I think that might be a good idea.

Maybe, I say. I could try.

Good girl, the midwife says.

Rosa is swooning in my arms with milk. I know there are other women waiting outside; I have taken up far more time than my ten-minute slot. I apologise for keeping her, but I don't want to leave the midwife. I don't want to have to cross a bridge and re-enter the world of speed and violence. I want the midwife to take me and Rosa home with her, to cook us a meal, to tuck us up in bed together, to show me how it might be possible to keep my baby safe. Mother me. Please. Mother me into mothering.

How are you feeling in yourself?

I repeat that question in my mind as I walk home with Rosa.

The quality of my thinking has changed. I have always been able to narrow down and zoom in on details; absorbed, consumed even, by the things my mind has fastened on to. But I used to be able to zoom back out too.

Right now, I'm walking down an alleyway in the Groves. Behind this alleyway, there's the long garden of a grand, Victorian, end-of-terrace house. There is wisteria behind this wall, which tumbles into the alleyway in summertime – long lines of lilac flowers falling over the terracotta bricks. When I passed the wall last summer, it made me think of a trip I took with my ex-boyfriend, Sol, to Italy, and the colours and sensations of being there – flowers draped down brickwork, suncream and espresso, the tight grip of a woman who had caught my wrist in a shop and threatened to call the police because I had refused to pay for something I had picked up and put back on a shelf when it was too expensive; how Sol and I had laughed at this, in the face of her threat, and, looking at those flowers, I was back in the tiny room Sol and I stayed in during that trip, the one holiday that we took together – he'd bought the flights as a surprise, but then couldn't make up the money to book accommodation, so I'd maxed a credit card to get the room for us, and the owner of the room left pastries outside the door for breakfast and a line of ants found the food each morning before Sol and I woke, and I was twenty-three and the world was expanding in every direction – up to the stars above the Santa Maria Novella and down to the ants, to wherever they took these little crumbs of sugar, under the brickwork of the Via della Scala, down into the intricate veins of subterranean life, through the loam and cherty limestone, the ants moving their breakfast between the bones of long-dead Tuscan plague victims and relics of ancient life.

All of this had expanded in my mind in a moment from those lilac flowers.

But now, as I pass the wall and try to remember how my mind used to work, there is only—

A vein rising in Rosa's neck. Her soft spot pulsing wildly. Is she too hot? Is she breathing right? How easily that vein in her throat could catch on something – my nail, the zip of her coat. How ruinously thin the membrane of my baby's life. Each detail in my visual field is a possible recrimination. I'm examining Rosa's body with forensic anxiety.

Back in the flat, as Rosa feeds, I google postnatal depression.

Baby blues: a dip in mood that is usual in the first two weeks post-partum. The rapid shift in hormones after giving birth is one of the most sudden and radical chemical changes a human being can undergo and feeling low is usual, all the websites say. But PND is longer lasting and more debilitating than the baby blues, or it occurs later. It is common for both mothers and fathers, and it is indicated by:

Low mood. I cry often now. My feelings sometimes lurch downwards as I hold or feed Rosa. But I don't feel low, exactly – there is no flatness to what I am feeling. In fact, maybe it's more accurate to say I feel high. My emotional life is lived at the top of staircases; above the river; staring down the shaft of a derelict lift. It's all vertigo.

Lack of enjoyment. I don't enjoy the things that used to bring me pleasure. I do not let myself drink alcohol because it might work its way into my breast milk and because it might make me drowsy and then I might fall asleep and crush the baby. I cannot watch TV: casual references to violence, even the standard, cynical modes of mainstream humour, are unbearable. I no longer enjoy eating – though my hunger and thirst outstrip anything in pregnancy – because the things that I see leave me nauseated. My enjoyment of Ryan is triangulated through the baby: we barely touch one another; we barely speak except to exchange information about Rosa. I cannot talk to my friends, because I have not worked out how to hold a conversation and still take care of the baby. And what would I say to my friends anyway? Some of them are pregnant and will need to hear that I'm doing well. Others have been desperately trying to become pregnant. Others are childfree and perhaps they knew best to stay away from this bloody business. And my friends who do have children – I realise now that I let go of them when their own children arrived; I have barely seen them since. I always send cards and expensive gifts for new babies, but

I never offer anything practical. Never even made a phone call. I always assumed that the best thing you could do for new parents was to send flowers and bunnies and leave them alone to get on with it. See you in a decade!

Lack of energy. Perhaps. Though I cannot sleep. My brain flickers, restlessly, through the night, and my body is restless too, wanting to move unencumbered by the baby, wanting to flee, and at the same time, thrumming with panic if I cannot feel the baby's heartbeat directly against my own. I have the kind of energy that a fever or bad trip brings.

Difficulty bonding with your baby. Define difficulty. The problem might be that I have sunk too far into Rosa, that I feel her abjection too keenly. More accurate to say: I find my baby's vulnerability triggering. I find my baby's total dependence triggering. I find the tiny glut of the vein in her throat, and the thinness of her skin, triggering. I find my baby's soft spot, and the proximity of her brain to hard objects, triggering.

Frightening thoughts. Yes. But this is more than *thoughts*. It is the deep knowledge in my body that something bad is coming towards us. The air crackling with static, the taste of metal filling my mouth.

Nothing in this diagnosis mitigates my fear for Rosa; nothing in the description of PND can explain my glimpses of our future.

How are my girls? Ryan asks when he returns from work. How was the weigh-in?

It was OK, I say. Her weight's improving. Tenth percentile now.

He fist-bumps the air and sweeps Rosa into his arms. I love you, our Rosa, he says to her, making his vowels northern. Yes, I do. Yes, I do.

Yes, he does. I see Ryan's love of our baby, and I envy it.

Ryan confessed to me, during our first week at home with Rosa, that he'd been afraid that he wouldn't love the baby when she arrived. He'd never spent any real time around infants; had no desire to hold them or breathe them in like other people seemed to have. But now that he'd met Rosa, he said to me, he loved her so much that it was like being *in love*. When he was out of the flat, he was waiting to get home – waiting to see her again, to hold her close, to smell her scalp, his heart beating with excitement.

The way Ryan loves our baby is ecstatic.

The way I love our baby is a total fucking disaster.

Ryan has Rosa in the crook of his arm, slow-dancing with her, as he likes to do. When he looks up at me, he stops in his tracks. Grace, he says. What's wrong? Did something else happen at the clinic?

I owe him some sort of explanation. I can't keep pretending that everything is just dandy while I secretly ship away the contents of the flat. I know that you're meant to share things in relationships, though this instinct does not come naturally to me. I should try to tell him what I've seen; I should let him know how precarious Rosa's life is.

Ryan is young, but he's survived difficult things. For instance: he told me, back on the boat, about 'the tunnel' that he's periodically entered since adolescence. He had to drop out of uni when things went *proper dark*. It took moving to the boat and being with the lads and playing guitar every day and a shit ton of lithium to finally sort him out. But he got through it.

And look at him now: swinging Rosa in his arms, deep in love with his baby, innocent of all the things that could happen to her.

No. I can't tell him what I've seen: he deserves to love Rosa like this, unfettered by grief, while we still have her.

I'll swallow my secret – like the terribly beautiful places, where the wind moans and the worst things are quilted under the earth.

It's nothing, I say. Hormones maybe. I'm due to see the doctor soon.

He tries to put his arm around me then, smooshing Rosa into his chest.

Grace, he says. Promise me that you'll talk to me. If things start getting . . . dark.

If things start getting dark. Jesus wept. What could be darker? Placental meat; purple vein pulsing at her throat; occult tissue of the brain throbbing at her soft spot.

I will, I say. And now I am a liar as well as the thief of Rosa's future.

In the deep panic hours of the night, Rosa's breathing changes. This time, I'm sure of it. Rosa hasn't slept at all – she cries any moment she isn't latched on, and I have been propped up in bed with her for hours. I tell myself she might be going through another growth spurt, cluster-feeding again. But as I listen to Rosa's breathing, I can feel it. It's not right. Something about how she swallows the air is different tonight.

I look at my phone: 03:26. I lie Rosa down in her crib and listen to her chest.

I Google *baby breathing difficulties* and I watch videos of children with croup and stridor. The alarm is rising in my body.

I have to shake Ryan to get him to rouse.

Ryan! I think something's wrong with Rosa's breathing. Will you come and listen to her?

Ryan is groggy, but he gets out of bed and comes round to my side.

Doesn't that sound off to you? I say.

I can't tell, he says. She always makes strange noises at night, doesn't she?

But is she struggling for breath? Look at her sucking in, here, around her collarbone. I think she's struggling for breath. And feel her forehead. Does she feel hot to you?

Ryan listens to her breathing for a while longer; places the back of his hand on her cheeks. Then he shrugs.

I'm going to ring one one one, I say.

I put the phone on to speaker. A nurse asks us a series of questions:

Has the baby been bleeding heavily? Has the baby ingested any poisons? Is the baby currently fighting for breath?

I think I'm going to be sick, I say to Ryan.

When I describe the rasping noise that the baby is making and the way I can see her ribs flare with each breath, the nurse puts us on hold.

When she returns, she directs us to an emergency clinic at the hospital.

I wrap Rosa in blankets inside the pram and we half-walk, half-jog round the deserted ring road towards the hospital.

Ambulances pass us, blue lights flashing, sirens silenced.

I pace in the waiting room holding my baby. I pace in the waiting room holding my baby. I pace in the waiting room holding my baby.

The doctor's eyes are red-rimmed. He's young and German and looks like he's at the tail end of a catastrophic night out. He asks me to undress the baby, then he pushes on Rosa's tummy and on the tops of her legs. He looks in her ears and her throat with a small light. He listens to her chest through a stethoscope.

I think, he says, after an agonisingly long stretch of silence, that your baby has a throat infection. I can see that her throat is swollen, so that's making it harder for her to breathe. But it's nothing serious. Nothing to worry about.

It's not a stridor, then? I ask.

No, the doctor says, the auscultation's fine. But you're right that she's drawing in around her collarbone, which means she's finding it harder work to breathe. You did the right thing bringing her in. Trust your instincts, he says, and always come in if you're worried.

Trust your instincts. Trust your instincts! Ha! I nearly laugh in the doctor's face. My instinct is that I want to be admitted. That I want me and Rosa to be admitted so that the doctor can watch us sleep, can monitor our every breath, the whole night through.

Outside the hospital again; bitter black cold February night.

What's stridor? Ryan asks as we walk back round the ring road.

Look it up, I say. I don't want to think about it again.

We push on in silence. Rosa, inside her sleepsuit and under three blankets, is finally sleeping.

It's starting to snow. Big flakes making shadows in the orange light of the street lamps.

Proper snow! Ryan says. This is her first real snowfall, isn't it?

The snowflakes drift around us, veering sideways and even upwards again in the orange light. The winter night is drawn close around us, the Minster in darkness, Rosa sleeping as the snowflakes land and then dissolve on her soft cheeks. The snow falling softly, muffling the city walls and the cobbled streets, blanketing the Vale of York.

Snuffing out the edges of the city. Dissolving on her soft cheeks.

I hear the rasp of a lighter. The fizz of a lit cigarette as it meets plump flesh.

No. The snowflakes are not falling softly. The snowflakes are falling on us like ash from a disaster zone.

*

I watch Rosa's breathing more closely than ever. If there is the slightest irregularity, if she gasps or pauses on the turn of her breath, which happens often, I strip her clothes to watch for the flare of her collarbones. I listen to the frantic beat of her heart with my cheek against her belly. Rosa's speeding heart makes my own heart flitter, when it's supposed to be the other way around. My heart, my breathing, should be settling my baby: instead, her palpitations are taking me over.

Ryan eyes me warily when I do this, when I strip Rosa to inspect her chest. He leaves me to it; he has begun to look afraid of me.

I discover that you can buy expensive sensor pads for your baby to sleep on. These pads claim to track your baby's heartbeat and rate of respiration in order to guard against Sudden Infant Death Syndrome. You can buy the same monitors that they use in hospital neonatal wards, which tell you if the baby's breathing *falls below a dangerous threshold*. I should have bought one of these sensors already. Maybe other parents track their babies this way. Just listening to your baby's breathing without proper apparatus now seems reckless.

Trust your instinct, the doctor said to me. Trust your instinct.

My instinct tells me that nothing good can come of this long winter. The earth has frozen hard again. When I walk with the pram through town, the cold slaps into the soles of my shoes and up into my bones. The days barely seem to get light and, when they do, the sun is low on the horizon and dazzling. Single magpies stalk me around the city. Black ice. Freezing fog. The trees appealing to the sky, leafless still.

My instinct tells me that only the bitterest things can ripen in a winter like this. Black olives. Dark-leafed vegetables that taste like a mouthful of earth. The white poison in mistletoe.

<error – excessive parameters>

My father has always looked uncomfortable when he comes to my flat. He's not made for domestic settings. He is forced to go inside for food and for sleep, but he always wants to be back out – on the beat, or to the pub, or walking up the valley – as quick as he can. Dad sits on my sofa with his hands on his knees. He looks the same as he did at the last visit: staring out of the window, waiting for a verdict to come in.

Lillian says that she'll make us tea. She's brought biscuits again and I know, from the way that Lillian says all this to me sotto voce, that I am being treated to a care visit.

When we're all sitting down, Lillian says: It must have been scary, Grace, having to take her to the hospital. My Jo had bronchiolitis when she was small. She was only about four months. It was awful. I remember it so well. But they're tougher than they look, you know.

Tough is meat in the mouth. Tough is leather. Nails and stone and steel. Tough has nothing to do with the soft, squirming creature in my arms. Her glistening eyes. Her wet and hungry mouth.

I sometimes wonder how long Rosa would survive if I put her down in the street and left her to fend for herself amid the cold and the crows. I reckon it would be less than a half-hour. The baby doesn't even have corvid-level intelligence yet – she couldn't use tools, for instance, and she has none of the crow's propensity for self-preservation.

Lillian is looking at me intently. We're worried about you, Grace. You don't seem yourself. Are you still not sleeping? You need to get the baby into a routine so that you can get some rest. Remember, sleep deprivation is a form of torture!

Lillian is making eyes at my father, but he stares resolutely ahead.

Look, Lillian says, when you're sleep-deprived, you can be pushed to your limits. I know. I remember the crying. It used to get right into my bones sometimes, just right into my skull. And if you ever feel like ... you might be about to lose it, you just walk away, Grace. You just put the baby in the cot and walk away. The baby will be fine left on her own for a few minutes. You don't want to get ... you don't want to get to the point where you might just lose it. Your dad had this case, remember, Pat, love? Terrible case. A while before, you know, *that case*.

Don't. Please don't talk about Baby S.

My father is white-knuckled on the sofa.

I hear, again, the rasp of a lighter.

Lillian carries on. This couple were at their wits' end. Their baby had colic, apparently, and the mother lost her rag, shook the baby, only for a moment she said, because she didn't know what else to do, and the baby was blind after that. They found this out weeks after it had happened, at a health visitor check. And when your dad went round, he found all sorts of stuff – the father worked for a vehicle recovery firm and he'd been stripping vehicles when there'd been a fatal accident, then selling on the parts. Nice little sideline. The living room was like a garage. Both of them went down, didn't they, Pat? And then the baby went up for adoption.

My father stands up suddenly.

Lillian, he says. These folk are nothing like our Grace.

All right, love, Lillian says. I didn't mean anything by it.

I want my father to say more. I want him to insist on my difference from these other people.

All I'm trying to say, Lillian says, is that it can happen to anyone. You can just lose it in the moment. Especially if you're sleep-deprived. I just want Grace to get some rest and to know that she can walk away from the baby. It doesn't always have to be like that – Lillian motions towards Rosa, latched on in my arms – surgically attached to her. It won't harm the baby to be left alone for a bit if Grace needs a breather.

My father comes over to me then and places a hand on my shoulder. He still smells of my childhood: soft leather jacket; spiced cologne; the white soap that he lathers on his hands – on his scuffed knuckles, to scrub them clean of dirt and blood.

We're here, he says. If you need us. If you need a break. I used to do some night-times, you know. If you wouldn't settle, or Isobel. Sometimes I couldn't get Isobel down, she was a right one, and I didn't want her screaming to wake you, so I'd drive out on the moortops till she went off, and then I'd just keep circling, round and round, until dawn. Lillian's right. Babies are tougher than they look.

Rosa's soft spot pulses, visible through her fine hair as she feeds. *Tough*. What a joke.

Whenever there's a well-publicised criminal case, people who have no connection to the crime come forward to confess to it. It happened with several of my dad's cases. A body was found in the

Huddersfield Broad Canal – this was two decades ago, when the canal was still an abandoned soup of plant life and shopping trolleys and stolen handbags. A middle-aged man had been stabbed and his body recovered from the water. There was a police appeal for witnesses, and a young man came forward. My dad told Nan about it over tea. *How has your day been, love?* Christine asks my father. Long pause as he takes his portion of bread-and-butter fingers. *It was a strange one today. You know that appeal we did? Well, we had a young lad in. Only seventeen. Comes in quietly, asks to speak to the detective in charge, then asks to be arrested. Please, he says to me, please will you lock me up? I did it. I stabbed him. Anyway, we run some background, and there's no obvious connection between the boy and this man. And when we talk to the lad, he can't give us anything specific about the man's injuries. He can't even tell us what the man looked like. He just says: I did it. I stabbed him. I stabbed him again and again and I pushed him in the canal. Poor lad. He was in a pitiful state. Pitiful.*

Now I understand. I want to confess. I want to plead guilty to my future crimes. Won't somebody please lock me up before any of the visions come to pass.

Anyway, Dad says. I've messaged your useless sister. It's about time she came across. Has she been in touch?

I check my phone: *Auntie Iz is coming to see you and this baby. Be there 3ish. Make sure she's looking especially cute xxx*

My father and Lillian leave, looking relieved to go, kissing Rosa on the forehead in goodbye.

And then there are just these walls, closing around me. The carpet, thickening under my feet. The teeth of the knives in the kitchen cupboards. The air ringing in here. The witness statement in the case review repeating in my mind: *The baby cries and cries, all hours of the day and night, the neighbour had reported. We haven't seen the mother in weeks.* Out of the window: the lime tree is leafless still, its branches splayed skywards like an exposed nerve.

I have a reason to get out of the flat, thank fuck. Isobel making this journey is a big deal: Marsden to York involves a bus and two trains and the chances of her making a connection and/or staying the course if she misses one are usually slim. Isobel once came to visit me at university and she arrived three days late absolutely destroyed: she'd lost her phone somewhere on the way, got off to seek help in London King's Cross and spent the next two days at a squat party on the Caledonian Road.

I message Iz to tell her that I'll meet her at the station. This plan has its drawbacks – it means I will have to cross either Lendal Bridge or the Scarborough Railway Bridge – but if I ask Isobel to make her own way into town, it's asking for trouble, and I need to see Isobel: I need her noise and chaos and total commitment to life in the present tense.

I walk into town, wheeling Rosa over the cobbles of the Shambles, her body juddering in the bassinet of the pram. I slow down, take the cobbles one at a time. One. Two. Three. If I were to continue at normal walking pace, I might pulverise some delicate connection inside her skull. I used to be the kind of person who walked rapidly and with purpose, frustrated by the meanderings of tourists and sightseers in York. Now, I've joined the population of drifters: those who stray through the city without the structure of a working day to discipline their movements. The elderly. The day-trippers. The destitute. The white-knuckled mothers. The homeless and the daytime drinkers of York, whom the city tries to hide with dispersal orders and ASBOs. In the cold, dark, early months of the year, small bunches of flowers keep appearing, sellotaped to shop windows with photographs and notes attached, only to be taken down by shop managers later the same day. This winter has been perilous for many.

I pass a woman who I see on the regular – she often sits outside the pharmacy on Monkgate waiting for her methadone. I've always assumed she's homeless, but I hear her talking on her mobile phone as I pass. I can't, the woman is saying. I can't *just go home*. You know I can't stay there now, ever since the police broke in and messed everything up, I feel like they're just going to burst in again. Any time they could come. No warning. When I've done nothing wrong, and Ashley hasn't lived with me for years. I can't hardly sleep there now, but the council won't listen. So no, I can't *just go home*.

As I stop to manoeuvre the pram over the edge of the kerb, a woman draws alongside me and peers in at Rosa.

Ah! she says. How old is she?

A new hazard in the city centre: strangers talk to you when you have a baby, especially older women. They veer towards you and they open doors for you and your pram. They ask questions about your baby's age and moral character – *Is she good? Is she good? Is she good?* – by which they mean does she eat and sleep well.

I tell the woman that Rosa is three months and then the woman tells me about her own twins, one of whom she lost to cancer in his twenties.

Oh, I'm so sorry, I say. And I am sorry, but I want to run away from this woman, whose grief is opening up like a sinkhole: nothing unusual to see at first, just a friendly old woman, peering into the pram, telling you that your baby is lovely, and then there's this ripple of remembrance, a landslip of sadness, widening and threating to suck you right in.

I wheel Rosa away down Parliament. There's a busker singing something melancholy, a number from a show: soaring grandiosity on this cold, pale day when the world is bleached of goodness. I glance into the pram to check on Rosa's breathing.

I stop dead.

Something unbelievable is happening in there.

Rosa's features are crushed together. Her face a total deformed squash-up.

She must be fitting, or suffering from some other internal catastrophe, conniption, aneurism, brain event.

No. That's not it.

I scoop Rosa out of her pram and into my arms.

My baby is smiling. Her first smile!

Again, I say to her. Again!

When the busker's song swells, Rosa bleats and then the flesh of her cheeks dimples in this unprecedented expression.

Her eyes are fixed on me. Rosa has become all smile, her whole body crushing into it.

My heart is about to shatter. I smile back at Rosa, my own face a crush of cheek and tears.

The busker continues to sing, and I put Rosa back into the pram. Ryan plays guitar to her sometimes in the evenings, and it often makes her shriek and mewl – noises at the cusp of delight and distress. Her tiny body flitters to the song now, her limbs jerking as though she is fitting with joy.

Rosa begins to whimper almost as soon as I arrive at the station. I know I can't touch her here. A train line is so much like a river – into which you could fall. On to which you could just tip a baby, spilling her open on the track. I am on the verge of walking back out of the station and counting home again when Isobel arrives on the platform.

You don't just look tired, Isobel says as we walk into town. You look smackhead grey.

Thanks, I say. It's good to see you too.

Ha! Isobel says. You know I'm always going to be honest with you. Is she really putting you through it then, my little niece? She must be, for Dad to finally message me. But look at her! Butter wouldn't melt.

It's true: Rosa seems happy as Larry in her pram now that we're walking. Maybe she likes Isobel's voice. And the light in the sky is different today: the hint of a new season in the future, a season that Rosa has never experienced.

We're walking back over the bridge, and I look away from Rosa as we cross the river, but it's easier not to focus on the depths when Izzy is at my side, chatting ten to the dozen about the dickheads at Marsden Station.

I'll need to feed her soon, I say. Could we sit down somewhere?

Yeah, yeah, course, says Izzy. Are you just going to … you know? Get your boob out in the middle of town?

Yeah, I say. I am. Because the baby needs feeding.

Cool, says Izzy. That's cool. Good on you. I mean, have you seen that Cardi B video? She just whaps it out and feeds her baby like a boss. Money, isn't it. Good on you.

Yeah, I say. I am just like Cardi B.

We sit together on a bench in the Museum Gardens. I'm getting slightly better at feeding in public – unhooking my bra, rearranging my clothing, positioning Rosa to get her to latch on as discreetly as possible. Though there are new challenges: Rosa is starting to look around. Sometimes she breaks off from feeding and just stares at the world around us, leaving me hanging. And it's cold still – cold air against my nipples, the shock of the outside hitting the intimate regions of my body. But soon Rosa has latched and the warmth of her mouth meets the warmth of my milk and then it is only my lips and fingertips that register the cold.

So, my sister says, I know it's taken me a while to get across to see you and this little one. But there's a reason for that. I was going to come this week anyway, even before Dad bollocked me. You're going to be pleased. You are. You're going to be dead pleased with me.

OK, I say. But listen, don't let Dad's message get to you. He's only—

Shut up! Isobel says. Shut up! You're spoiling my big reveal.

Go on then, I say.

It's quite hard to focus when I can see your massive boob out the corner of my eye. But anyway, I knew you'd be worried about any crazy stuff happening around the baby. And maybe your Ryan would be too—

That's not true, I say.

Ryan hasn't expressed a single concern about Isobel.

Shush, Iz says. Whatever you say, I know no one wants chaos around a baby. Anyway. Anyway, I've been working really hard. Six weeks, Grace, and I haven't touched owt. Not even a bit of spliff! Seeing this little one has been my motivation. Hurry up feeding, baby, Auntie Izzy wants a cuddle.

Iz looks good. Her nails are painted bright red: neat and glossy. She smells good too. Her hair falls down her back – dark roots brightening to orange at the tips.

When Rosa has finished feeding, I hand her over and Iz is made up. She rocks Rosa, and then goes mega mooshy, making silly sounds into the baby's ears. The baby scrutinises her, then turns on her smile: a proper full-faced conniption, just like before.

Rosa dimpling in my sister's arms, that crush of joy: I jam the heels of my hands against my eyes.

She's only just started doing that, I say. I think that's her second smile.

I want one, Isobel says. Aw, man. I honestly think I do.

We go to a café for lunch. Izzy jiggles Rosa while I eat and I instruct Izzy to support Rosa's head and I show her where the baby's soft spot is and how to avoid it.

All right, all right, Izzy says. I have held babies before, you know. I spent loads of time with Maria's two, probably changed more nappies than she did.

OK, I say.

I don't say: *But Maria's two were taken into care for a while, because Maria accidentally set herself alight when she was drunk at a party with you and ended up in hospital and told the nurses the kids were home alone, and it took several days for Maria's parents to discover this and then to get them back, so maybe Maria wasn't the best teacher where babies are concerned.*

Still, Iz is holding Rosa safely and it is good to have two hands free to lift a burger, and I need to eat – I need to eat to keep my milk up.

When I've finished my food, my sister hands Rosa back to me.

I'm going for a wazz, Iz says. And do you know what? I'm not even taking my bag. So you know for sure. Clean as a whistle, that's me.

Isobel's bag remains on the floor beneath our table. Once she's out of sight, I push the neck of it open with my foot. A purse, a phone, a lipstick, and a roll of banknotes secured with an elastic band. Two miniatures of vodka, unopened. It does look surprisingly clean, but the money worries me. Why would Iz have this much on her in cash if she isn't buying or selling—

Right, Iz says, sitting back down at the table. Let's go and get a drink and then you can tell me what's up with you, and why Dad thinks things are so bad that I need to visit *urgently*, and why you look so bloody mournful when you've got this beautiful bouncing baby.

We buy takeaway coffees from the Shambles Market. Iz retrieves one of the miniatures from her handbag and laces hers with vodka.

What? Don't look at me like that! I'm clean, but I'm not a fucking saint.

I'm not judging her. Not in the way she thinks. I'm wondering how we've ended up like this. Me: now terrified of a sip of alcohol, terrified of bridges, of stairs, of the teeth of a can-opener and the unpredictable energy of my own shaking hands. And her: totally fucking dauntless.

So come on then, says Iz as we're walking. What's so fucking terrible then, Grace? Is it Ryan? Or are you messed up, *down there*, after the birth? I know folk don't want to say if their vagina's been totally destroyed but you can tell me. I know someone who had that mesh stuff used to fix her back together, there's always something you can do. You know you can tell me anything—

It's not that, I say.

What then? she says. Come on. I'm listening, Grace.

Can I tell her what I've seen?

I don't know, I say. I think ... something bad is about to happen. To Rosa, I mean.

Like what?

Like, I keep thinking that she's going to stop breathing, I say.

But she's healthy, right, Iz says. You had her checked over at the hospital when she was breathing funny, didn't you. That's what Dad told me, in his first text message in five years: *The baby's grand, but you need to check in on my beloved first-born daughter*, something like that. But there's nothing wrong with her, Grace. Look at her.

Rosa is squirming happily in my arms.

I've heard this can happen, though. Maybe you've got a touch of the dreads.

The dreads?

Yeah, you know, that anxious feeling when you're coming down and your body's draining, and the whole world's going dark, and you start worrying about every little thing: like, did I really say that to that girl last night, oh, Christ, she's going to hate me, and did I pay that bill or are they going to send the bailiffs, and where is my fucking passport, I haven't seen it for months, and what about work next month, no one's ever going to give me another job, and why would they, I'm an unreliable dickhead, and I keep getting headaches and I never did buy a carbon monoxide detector because I'm fucking useless, and of course my dad doesn't want to see me, why would he, and everything good that is ever going to happen to me had already happened by 1997, and there's only bad stuff to come now: you know, that sort of feeling. The dreads. It would make sense to get it after giving birth, when you're all over the place with hormones. Massive crash and the sleep deprivation and all that. Maybe it's harder for you because you're usually so on top of everything. It's not gonna last. You've just got to ride it out.

Maybe, I say.

But *the dreads* doesn't come close to the static in my body and the ringing in the air, and my mounting certainty that I am only a heartbeat away from some terrible act against Rosa or myself.

Have you seen Mum? Iz asks.

No, I say. She's gone dark again.

It might be good, Iz says. You know, useful. To see her.

Useful? I say. Dad says she can't handle babies. Literally – can't hold them. So I don't know about useful.

I don't mean in that way, Isobel says. I'm not saying she's going to be dead hands on or anything. I just mean, she obviously went through something, after we were born.

Maybe, I say. But she's never wanted to talk about it.

No, says Iz. But just – I don't know. It might be good for both of you.

Yeah, or it might push her right over the edge, I say.

Over the edge. All fall down. Motherless. No one to kiss our knees; or hers. No one to stop this terrible plunge.

I don't tell Isobel about the grief that grips me deep in the night. A hunger, as I nurse Rosa, for a form of care that we never knew.

Back at the flat, we sit on the sofa while I feed Rosa. Isobel is now swigging vodka straight from the bottle.

God, it takes ages, doesn't it, Isobel says. I thought feeding a baby would just be, like, a few minutes, and then you're off.

Yeah, same, I say. I had no idea. It takes absolutely hours. And sometimes, when she's finished feeding, I try to stand up and I actually can't. My legs go wobbly. It feels like she's sucking the marrow directly from my bones.

Ha! says Isobel. Don't you want to try bottles, to give yourself a bit more freedom?

Maybe, I say.

I've googled this, of course, but bottles aren't easy either. All the sterilising and preparation and making sure you take everything with you wherever you go and choosing the best kind of formula. And then you've got to teach the baby how to take the bottle, but manage it so that it can still breastfeed, if you want it to do both. Nipple confusion is a risk – then the baby can't navigate between teat and breast.

Honestly, I say, I don't think I've got it in me to master something new right now.

That's not like you, Isobel says. I thought you'd be devising spreadsheets for feeding times. Or there's probably an app now, isn't there. What do you do, while you're feeding her? I'd go mad just pinned there.

I don't really know what I do, I say. I thought I'd read stuff, but I can't. I'm too tired and sometimes I can't get to my phone in time. I can't even watch things on TV now. I find everything . . . I don't know. Like yesterday, I switched it on and it was a talk show, and there's a section about spring trends, and then there's an interview with a woman whose son's been stabbed to death. Stabbed in the throat. I can't take that stuff now. So when I've got my phone handy, I just google things. You know, to try to find out how to look after a baby. I stalk Facebook groups about parenting.

OK, Isobel says. Well, that'll do it. No wonder you're getting depressed. Shall we put some music on? Babies like music, don't they?

Isobel finds something she likes on the radio – a song from the '90s that sounds both naively hopeful and hopelessly melancholic. She starts wheeling round the living room.

Come on, she says, you can have a little dance too, it'll be good for you. I bet you can manage that with her still latched on and all.

Standing up with a baby latched on is a challenge, but I manage it – rocking backwards until I have the momentum to rise, hands free, from the sofa – and I find that it is possible to dance with the baby.

My sister is whooping and twirling. Tiny flecks of her rolling tobacco are being disseminated across the carpet and furniture with each of her movements. She's half-cut now.

The music swells. I went to see this band live once. It was in a field in London, and the air was warm and vibrant with skunk. I was there with friends, and we danced and sang and leant against one another and howled into the sad bits.

How did I ever do that: listen to music for pleasure; birth-love-hope-joy-loss compacted into two and a half minutes for recreational purposes.

I look at Rosa in my arms.

Her cheeks are dimpling again. That little seizure of a smile. I feel the bare, bright life of her, my vital organ.

And I watch as she spills from my arms.

As her head hits the coffee table, her soft spot gouged by the sharp corner.

The music swells. Rosa is safe in my arms.

I'm going to change her, I say to Isobel, and I leave my sister swaying in the living room while I count my way to the bathroom.

*

Later that evening, when Ryan arrives home, Isobel says that she's heading off.

I'll leave you two to it, she says. Bedtime, bath-time, all that cosy shit.

She's been distracted by her phone for a bit.

Where are you going? I ask.

There's a mate who lives not far from here. Poppleton, is it? She's going to come into town and meet me. She's got little ones too and it sounds like she's absolutely gagging for a night out.

Right, I say. Are you coming back here, after?

I don't want to disturb you, she says. I might be late. I can crash at hers.

I can give you a key? I say.

Nah, you're all right, she says. I'll get out of your hair.

Isobel leans in to hug me.

I begin to cry then, and I can't make it stop.

I'm not sure I've ever cried in front of Isobel, at least, not after the age of nine. Not after our mother left. Not even when our nan died. I hid my face from Isobel at the funeral, to prevent my sister from seeing me falter.

Don't leave me alone with the baby, I whisper to her. Please.

Isobel looks at me with a new expression: a stutter in her perception of me – a double-take.

Grace, Isobel says. Man. Grace, it's OK. Right, give over, you're making me want to cry and I don't even know why we're crying.

She hugs me.

OK, OK. Give me this key. I'll come back. But it won't be early. All right?

I tell Ryan about Rosa's smile. We try to make her do it again, Ryan peek-a-booing from behind his hand, and when she does, dimpling up, Ryan's face is a total crush too. Again! Again! He gurgles with laugher.

When I get Rosa ready for bed that night, when I bathe her and spread cream on her bottom and over her warm body, I do not allow myself to touch her in any of her tender places – where the skin is so thin, I can see her tiny veins, rising close to the surface.

Rosa's wrists and her throat and the backs of her knees.

The small jugular clot beneath the chub of her chin.

The soft spot on her head, pulsing.

I've heard stories about people removing their own aching teeth in extremis. Perhaps I could do something similar: drill through my own skull to gouge out whatever bit of my brain makes me see her being harmed. Anything. I'd do anything to make this stop.

As I lie down in bed next to the Moses basket that evening, even the thought of one more night like this is unbearable.

So, I make a new rule:

If I accidentally touch Rosa in one of her tender spots, if I feel even the slightest spasm of movement towards her, I will take Rosa somewhere safe, and then I will disappear.

Abandoned. In my own family, there have been at least two literal instances of abandonment. A baby swaddled in a scarf and placed in a handbag in a phone box in the centre of Bradford. That baby was my maternal great-grandmother, and, though I never met her, I know that she was adopted and loved. And on my father's side, there is a story about a baby wrapped in furs and placed in a rabbit warren at the edge of a large estate, close enough to workers' cottages to be easily discovered when it cried. People speculated that the mother was a lady or in service at the big house. The baby was brought up by a working family in the village and became part of my father's great-uncle's family. Abandoned. No. That word feels unjust. These babies were left carefully. Left swaddled in the hope of something better.

Perhaps that's what Mum did too. Leaving me – and Isobel – in the hope of better care. *Nan will take care of you*, she said to us on one of those contact visits, when she hugged us close in desperate bursts, the hug lasting too long, Mum beginning to shake and cry as she breathed into our hair. *Nan will take care of you much better than I ever could.*

I know now: if I touch Rosa in one of her tender places, if I even feel tempted to touch her there, then I will take Rosa somewhere safe. I will leave her at the Minster doors on a busy morning, swaddled tight. And then, because I know that I cannot live without her warm, pulsing life, I will finish my own.

There is the river. I could river myself away. Or there are the blades that I have hidden in cupboards.

I am back in that hot bath that the midwife drew for me after the birth: I feel myself enter the water again, and in this new water my blood flows like it did after Rosa's birth, the blood beating out of me so richly – and the blood flowing into this new water means that my baby is alive, my baby will remain alive, while life rivers out of me, everything I have seen rivering out of me, so that my Rosa remains safe from harm.

The perfection of this image, the feeling of my life flowing freely and warmly out of me, is beyond premonition. It feels like deliverance. I am already dead, this winter night, lying in the darkness next to Rosa and carried away by water.

Never mind rivering. Once upon a time you learned to fly. You learned to soar above your fears, to follow the meadow pipits over the moortops.

Here you are, leading Isobel through the corridors of secondary school. The air is thick with the scent of synthetic vanilla and sexual threat. At first, you learn new fears here. You are taught about the dangers of electricity pylons and teenage pregnancy and choking on your own vomit after drinking. In history class, you are shown video footage from a concentration camp – a grainy film of bodies heaved into a mass grave. This really happened, the teacher says. And it could happen again. Then the bell rings and you move on to the next lesson. In 'Skills' class, the girls from your year are taken to a Portakabin and told about toxic shock syndrome. The year head dangles a tampon in front of you from its string, like a mouse from its tail. If you use a tampon, she tells you, this *supposedly* hygienic object might trigger bacteria in your body to poison your blood. This snug little thing might finish you off. She snatches the tampon away. Pads are safer, she says, though they bring their own challenges. Remember, girls: you can never mask a smell with another smell. There are whole assemblies devoted to that hysteria of secondary schools in the 1990s: Ecstasy. The police come in to tell you all about bad batches of pills in the area. Recovered drug addicts come in to tell you about losing their teeth and all contact with their families. You're repeatedly shown pictures of Leah Betts in a coma after she took a pill on her eighteenth birthday. Ecstasy will make your brain swell. Ecstasy will make you drink litres of water, until you drown yourself from within.

We followed the rules together, Isobel and I. But as our fears multiplied, they overspilled. The experience of fear – that high-pitched drone in the air, the taste of metal in our mouths – became an appetite. No way out but through. We began to pursue the very things that had haunted us. We couldn't have told you that was what we were doing, but Isobel and I followed our senses, which recognised danger whenever we were in striking distance; our teenage bodies thrummed at its resonating frequency.

Walking home from school a car slows down beside us. Two lads from town are slouched in the front seats. Our stomachs flutter; our pulses tick. These boys do not pay us compliments, but they drive steadily alongside us, and they have good tunes going. They offer us some drinks. We drive up to the moortops with them, where they roll us joints and teach us to hold the smoke in our mouths, and we laugh and gulp at the air, and cosy up with them when the sun begins to set and the wind scores through the heather. Then they drop us back at the edge of the estate and promise to come back soon.

The lads return in different cars each time and bring us gifts – booze, and jewellery in little boxes from H. Samuel. We sneak out to meet them, and they drive us, drunkenly, at speed along the road that runs through the valley bottom, all the way through to Saddleworth. They'd take us out in Manchester, they said, when we were a bit older, though you had to be careful there because of the CCTV. Once, we were in a car with them and Liam, the driver, smashed into a parked van – our car spun in the middle of the road, and when it came to a stop, Liam opened his door and fell right out onto the tarmac. Then he tore off on foot, shouting back at us: Scram! Fucking scram! Liam had done time in a young offenders' institute for twocking. He wasn't about to go back again. We stumbled out together, Isobel and I, dazed and laughing. Isobel was sick a little later, but still we laughed as we ran down the road, away from the scene. What about the hooch? Isobel said suddenly, pulling up, panting. We ran back together then to ransack the car for valuables. If we worried, in the sober light of day, about internal injuries and the police, we needn't have: neither materialised. We felt newborn from our fears, that night: we couldn't sleep for hours. We kept remembering the spinning sensation, and Liam falling over, and it made us giddy again with laughter.

I took Liam to Titanic Mills. He parked up by the canal and we walked beside the silent water together and the moon was bright in the sky above us. It was easy to get inside – there'd been a spate of Mill-stripping burglaries, and the boarding on the ground-floor windows had been broken away. The Mill stank of decades of damp and pigeon shit, but Liam laid his coat on the floor and he said something reverent to me before we lay down together: Grace, he said, I'll stay with you for ever, if you want me to. Then, thinking better of it: Or, like, at least until the end of the summer. I didn't care what he said; or rather, I wanted him to say nothing. In the darkness, my body was moonlight, and the wind through the valley and my breath came in hysterical snatches, as though I was being buried alive, as though I was being buried in the earth of this valley, and then I was screaming. I shattered into glass, into broken starlight, on that Mill floor in the darkness.

After that, I went with Liam to all the forbidden places: we drove up over the Pennines to Dovestones Edge and the Boggart Stones. We got high together in those desolate spots as the sky turned violet and the meadow pipits dipped between grass and sky, sky and grass.

And then I was hungry for more.

I sensed which boys, and then which men, might hurt me. Being able to recognise this was a sixth sense that Isobel and I shared. It often *was* the quiet ones, the ones who looked at you in a magnetised way, a string inside me vibrating then, theremin high. I was drawn to boys who liked to strangle me and threaten me into climax, and then to men who left lighter burns on my arms and wrists. I took whatever substances were offered to me – especially the things we'd been warned against at school: hard liquor and Ecstasy. I rode the wave of fearful nausea all the way through to rushing pulsing brimming-over bliss.

I was chasing the things that terrified me; I was surviving the things that terrified me.

We were not careful then, Isobel and I. We no longer needed to be careful. We were flying wild and high as the skylarks, over derelict furnace chimneys and sawtooth roofs, over wrecked mills and drystone walls, all the way up to the moortops, and up, further still: we soared over Wessenden Reservoir, we soared over Dovestones Edge, over the bodies that lay buried there, over all of the trembling children consigned to the earth, up and over all the most terribly beautiful places.

My heart is hammering in my chest as Rosa whimpers in the cot beside me. My throat fills with the possibility of sound; of calling out. I turn and muffle myself into the pillow. I am not crying in self-pity: I am crying at the deep, obscene relief of that thought of rivering myself – of my life turned to water and blood.

The bed next to me is empty. Ryan must have moved to sleep on the sofa.

Remember. Remember how to. Soar. Wind through the valley. Heather flattened to earth. Smashed glass. Bright moon. Fearless.

I am back inside the night that I first met Sol, outside the pub in Marsden, the drink and the cold making me jitter, the valley black and deep around us, the wind scouring across the moortops, someone playing acoustic guitar inside the pub, and Sol's mouth is hot and deep when we find each other, in the alleyway at the side of the pub. *I've loved you for so long*, he says to me. *Did you know?* I had not known.

I listen for the distant pulse of traffic. I wait for cold dawn at the window.

Interminable night-time.

I am already drowned, this winter night, lying in the darkness next to Rosa, entering that imaginary river. I'm on the other side. And yet my heart is hammering in my chest. My pulse surges at my throat.

Remember: once upon a time, you learned to fly. Remember.

<system overwrite>

The morning is bright and lucid. I scoop Rosa up from her cot and go in search of Isobel. She's fully clothed, asleep on my sofa, her mouth agape. The living room is chaos – the contents of Isobel's bag are spread all over the floor, along with two big bottles of pop and an empty vodka bottle. But she's come back. I settle into the comfy chair to feed Rosa and I listen to my sister's breathing.

Where is Isobel, when will she come home, is Isobel safe?

Isobel and I flew wild together. We sped up the valley in the same stolen cars, we necked the same hooch, inhaled the same smoke, ingested the same pills. But at a certain point, our paths diverged.

It is possible to be jaded by the time you're fifteen. Here you are, back at Titanic Mills – a cold night at the end of spring, the thick walls are cave-like with damp, that stink of mould, and you're with a boy who's rolling joints for you and Isobel, telling you about parties in Manchester, telling you about new drugs – G, liquid Ecstasy – and how he can get some for you, and how his cousin runs the doors in town and he can get you into the Visage any time you want. But you don't want. He kisses sloppily and you're bored.

I had pursued my deepest fears without serious injury. I had been to the forbidden places and lived to tell the tale and the thrill of the things that Isobel and I did together had begun to blunt. I was tired of driving to the same desolate places with the same boys. I didn't want to spend the rest of my life threatened into orgasm at the bottom of the Colne Valley.

It was then that I fell into books. Our nan, Christine, gave me her copy of *Rebecca*, and I read it as I ate my breakfast, I read it on the bus to school, I kept it in the pocket of my winter coat and I read it in the cloakroom at break time.

Whenever I read, I fell completely into the world of whichever book I was reading. I dreamt I went to Manderley again, and the woods crowded, dark and uncontrolled, around me – the beeches with white, naked limbs leant close to one another, making a vault above my head like the archway of a church. Next, I lived at 124, which was spiteful. Full of baby's venom. I watched a knife cut my thumb instead of an onion. What a thrill. The sweat was lashing oafay Sick Boy, who wis trembling. I tried no tae notice the cunt. He wis brining me doon. I watched the moths fluttering among the heath and harebells; I listened to the soft wind breathing through the grass. My soul swooned into some new world, fantastic, dim, uncertain as under sea. I was near to the wild heart of life.

I stayed up late at night, reading in total absorption. Then I began to write about what I was reading. I found that I was able to process words and facts and arguments at adrenaline speed, and I was able to write at adrenaline speed too. I memorised facts for exams in a glorious panicky rush and I drilled myself with quotations, until they became my catechism. The English teacher at school took me to one side and gave me extra reading and exam questions. I aced my GCSEs and then they wanted me to take five A levels, so I did. I was reading and writing all the time. I was writing essays that were thousands of words long, essays that my teachers sometimes could not read because my handwriting became illegible with speed. My thoughts were running wild and I was drowning in books, coming up only occasionally for big gulps of physical world, then going under again.

My teachers began to seem perturbed by me. But I was producing work that was brilliant: my grades were the highest in my year and my school needed my A level points. But how was I writing so much and when was I writing it? Was everything OK at home? my personal tutor asked. Was everything OK with my sister? Because Isobel was not doing well at school. Isobel was hardly there, in fact. She was bright, her teachers said to our nan at parents' evening, but she was becoming a troublemaker. She fell out with her female friends regularly and had violent altercations in the girls' loos. She'd been excluded for truanting – which seemed counter-intuitive. Why banish someone who doesn't want to be at school? While I was falling into books, Isobel was falling for a risibly minor gang player who supplied skunk to the disaffected teens of the valley. While I was cramming at night, Isobel was out with Sean, helping him to make his deliveries to Slaithwaite and Marsden. A pretty local lass popping into a pub or hanging out in a park was less of a cause for suspicion than a thirty-three-year-old man with a distinctive scar running down the right-hand side of his face. By the time she was sixteen, Isobel had developed a speed habit and would do anything Sean asked of her.

When Isobel was first arrested, she told the officers our father's name and rank, and she got off with a caution. A police officer brought her home and spoke with our father in the kitchen. Dad thanked him as he left. Good man, he said, good man. I won't forget this.

Dad served us with an ultimatum then. He served it with white-cold rage: his lips blanched, his cheeks pitted, his eyes unable to meet ours.

I can't protect you if you do stupid things out there. Stay out of trouble or leave.

Isobel left.

Isobel went to stay with our Auntie Janet while she finished her GCSEs. Then she stayed with the family of a school friend over the summer holidays. After that, it became more difficult to keep track of her. We'd speak on the phone, but Isobel was often evasive. *Yeah, I'm just with some mates for a bit.* Which mates, where, for how long? Can I come and visit? There would be laughter and voices in the background, voices that I didn't recognise. *Nah, Grace, you don't know them. You wouldn't like it here. We're moving on soon anyway.* Are you OK? Are you OK, that was all I ever needed to know, but there was never a straight answer. It was always all about the next thing: *Yeah, yeah, we're going to be grand. We're going to buy this van and travel to festivals together. We're going over to stay in Manchester for a bit. Yeah, yeah, I can't talk about it on the phone, but we've got something big planned this summer. And then I'll be set up for the next year at least.*

Every so often, there'd be a distress call. Isobel would phone me needing money to tide her over, *just until . . .* Or things would get out of hand with the speed. She'd call up crying then. No words. Just sobbing on the line, gasps, and then: *Sorry, Gracie. Sorry. Sorry.* I would try to get to wherever Isobel was. Once, I collected her from a house in Leeds where all the windows were covered with grilles. There was a small camera positioned above the door, trained on me. When I knocked, some bloke on the other side shouted: *What the fuck do you want?* And I replied: *Isobel.* After a few moments the door opened just enough for Iz to slide out. She slumped straight down on the steps and the door slammed shut behind her. Then it reopened and her rucksack was thrown out. Iz was shaking and her skin had a green, amphibious quality. Her speech was slurred. I called a taxi, and the driver laid out the schedule of fees for vomiting in the car but agreed to drive us back to York, where I was living in a bedsit on the Hull Road. I tried to put Isobel to bed, but she would not stay there. She wouldn't eat. She would only drink Lucozade. She couldn't sleep. She was slow but somehow still wired. *Shall we try to watch a film or something?* I suggested. *You need to get me some ketamine,* Isobel said. *Get me some fucking ketamine. It'll knock me out, and when I come round, I'll be fine. Honestly. I've done it before. You'd only need to check I was breathing every few hours. Please, Grace. Please. Get some ket for me.* I had no idea where to get ketamine in York and I was too scared to put Isobel under anyway. I gave her vodka instead, until she slept, which she then did for several days, waking only to inhale pizza and fizzy drinks before going under again. When Iz was back on her feet, she swore off speed and headed back to Huddersfield to start over.

I rang Isobel every night after that. I messaged her for her location. I wanted her to tell me her movements, and what she was ingesting, and to message to let me know that she'd woken up safely after every big night out. Years and years of trying to keep track of my sister. I should have kept my eye on her long before all this. It was my fault; I'd left her alone when I went off with Liam, the very first boy who'd driven us on to the moortops, with his mate, not thinking about her, not thinking she was younger than me – thinking only about my own desire to speed up and over the valley tops.

When things were bad with Isobel – when I couldn't track her down, or when she needed rescuing from a squat or a bender – people at work, who only saw their families at Christmas and for prearranged pub lunches, counselled me on healthy relationships: *You need to establish clear boundaries. There's only so much you can do for someone. She'll never learn if you keep stepping in.* I decided that I had to give up worrying about Isobel. She lived in a different way from me, and she didn't want to be saved from anything. I knew that Isobel looked at my life – my job and my little flat and my friends who didn't intrude on me or claim my sofa as theirs – and found it dull and sanitary. I made myself turn away from her.

Now, I watch my sister sleeping on the sofa. She smells sour and familiar. I listen to her breath, alert for drunken, silent vomiting.

When she wakes, she groans. Water, she says, her mouth gummy.

You'll have to get it yourself, I say. I'm feeding the baby.

Ugh, says Isobel. Kick me that bottle then.

I use my foot to roll the bottle of pop towards her.

Isobel opens the cap to bleed the fizz out, like she always does, then drinks the bright orange liquid.

Right, she says. This is what we're going to do.

She has it all planned. Her friend, Natalia, has convinced her that I have postnatal depression and she doesn't really care what I say, she is taking me straight to the GP this morning.

In the deep of the night, I had perceived my own imminent death as a kind of spell. And this morning, here I am, walking with my baby and my sister, looking to all the world like a functioning new mother. The crocuses have given way to daffodils and narcissi in the verges. For a moment, I appreciate the beauty of the clear blue sky above me; the cloud of my breath; the bright tissue of spring flowers emerging from the earth. I know, in the cold light of this morning, that death isn't enchanting. That death is not water and blood and flowers: that suicide is no Millais painting. I've heard enough from my father about the stink and the bloat and the waste and the mess of death.

From now on, I am living in two worlds.

In one, I have seen the future, and it has already swept me away, cold and swift and deadly.

In the other, I am trying, by the light of day, to make sense of what I am seeing; I am trying to remember how to fly.

Make sure you tell the doctor how bad it is, right, Isobel says. I know what you're like. Don't put a brave face on it. Tell her you're not sleeping. Tell her about the dreads and the crying and all of that. You've really got to ramp things up to get any support, you know.

I have no idea what I will say to the doctor. What's the matter, you ask, doctor? Well, the matter is that I've seen the future. The future is singing its dark song right through me.

Isobel says she'll wait with me at the surgery – as though she thinks I might be planning to do a bunk. But I'm not going to bolt: I'm too afraid to spend another night alone with what I've seen.

The doctor is a kind and worried-looking woman. She'll do the six-week check on the baby while we're here, she says – we're very late doing it, she apologises for that – and then we'll talk about *you*. She settles the cold drum of the stethoscope against Rosa's belly and then against her chest. She checks Rosa's limbs. She unfastens Rosa's nappy and lifts her legs.

Lovely, the doctor says. Everything is looking great. You're doing a great job.

I break down then.

She asks me a series of questions, and I answer each of them with a nod or a shake of my head. No, I can't sleep. No, I don't enjoy the things I used to. No, I don't have a history of mental ill-health.

All right, the doctor says. Last question. This is a hard one. Do you ever think you might harm yourself? Do you ever make plans to?

I can't explain to this kind, worried woman the obscene relief of the image of my body rivering out of life.

I shake my head.

The doctor issues me a prescription for antidepressants, along with several warnings about side effects. But I will try anything, now, to blunt what I've seen.

I can understand, in the deep of those first few medicated nights, why people believe in the Devil.

The medication makes me grind my teeth. My whole body is set on edge. I drift between sleep and wakefulness, the nightlight in the bedroom making everything crime-scene, luminol blue. When I walk with Rosa towards the bathroom, the corridor is so long and black, tunnelling me towards the winding staircase, where this all began, and I am walking with Rosa in a dream, I am walking with Rosa in a nightmare, I am letting her go, and she is falling. I can't breathe then.

Something is trying to possess me. Every building in York is constructed on the ruins of ancient devastation. The Sainsbury's car park, just below this flat, conceals beneath it a medieval Jewish cemetery. There's a small plaque, commemorating the hundreds interred there. I read that inscription years ago and barely thought about it, but now, in the dead of night, the whine I hear through the wind, through my skull, is the murmuring dead beneath the tarmac and the shopping trolleys. Nameless children and mothers – centuries, millennia, of women and their infants buried in this city. I feel the proximity of evil: little spasms of destruction through my jaws and hands. I count and I turn the ring on my finger, trying to ward off these grieving, restless mothers, trying to fold myself into unconsciousness.

Ryan's voice is thick with sleep when he asks if I am OK. In the night, his face has altered. Any man can turn, if pushed. His skin is blue. His features have been swallowed by the darkness, his eye sockets turned to blind shadow. He's owned by the night-time now; he could stalk alleyways, could stalk the moortops, burying his secrets there.

I roll away, so I don't have to look at him. Go back to sleep, I tell him. I'm OK.

The mornings are grey and indistinct. I get dressed, I pour milk on to cereal, I change Rosa's nappy. I google *antidepressants and infanticide* and then throw my phone across the room before any headlines can load.

I fear the drugs entering my breast milk. The baby shouldn't even ingest water or juice at this point; how is her tiny body going to cope with the drugs, and what effect will they have on her soft little brain? I've read the articles about *the first thousand days* – a baby's first three years are crucial for their development and much of the brain's architecture and patterns are determined in this *precious, formative* time. I am fucking up the first thousand days for sure.

Astonishingly, my sister is a voice of total calm.

Grace, she says, these drugs are mild mild mild. And they start you off on a tiny amount. Natalia told me it's just like taking your vitamins. You need to do it if the doctor says so. And they're super cautious about pregnant and breastfeeding women, they hardly let you take *anything*. So, if the doctor says it's OK, it really is OK.

But the doctor said I shouldn't be alone, I say. In the first few weeks on the medication. In case ... I don't know.

All right, Isobel says. Yeah, well, I'll stick around then. For a bit. Until you're settled. You'll have to lend me some clothes though. I stink already.

Once upon a time, you learned to fly high, up over the moors. Try. Trying to remember. How to follow the skylarks, to soar above your fears.

The doctor has asked me to call a self-referral number for talking therapy.

If it was hard to call, she told me, she could ask the health visitor to come round and help—

Anything to avoid the health visitor and her litany of ways to kill an infant.

So I call the number. I am told that ex-military personnel and new mothers are priority cases, and that I'll be seen within the week.

I am terrified of the talking therapy. And I am terrified of not doing the talking therapy. Try. Trying to. I know I can't bear these visions for much longer. I'm liable to gouge out my own mind's eye.

An old chapel, secreted behind the hospital, now houses Psychological Medicine. I am encouraged by the sacred appearance of the building. I am hoping for a wise-looking woman who has seen *everything* and cannot be shocked, someone with the remit of a priest, or a shaman, or a witch. I am after someone who can perform an exorcism, who can reckon with and change the course of my baby's future.

Instead, my therapist, Francesca, is young and nicely dressed and painfully attentive. She ushers me into a small, tidy room.

She talks me through my scores on the questionnaires that were sent to me ahead of our session. She tells me that she is glad I have come here to get some support. She asks me about Rosa's birth.

I don't know what I can tell her. I'm here under false pretences, with my healthy, *thriving* baby and my recovering body, after my dream of a birth. I have a partner who loves our baby, and I have maternity pay and a job to return to. I should not be wasting this therapist's time and valuable NHS resources. Instead, I should be somewhere sacred making offerings to the magpies that circle me and Rosa. I should be with a fortune teller or a tarot reader: someone else who can see what I've seen.

Rosa starts to cry.

I might need to feed her, I say.

That's OK, Francesca says. And then, after a few moments, when Rosa has latched on: Is it OK if I ask you some questions?

Francesca asks about my history of mental ill-health. When I tell her that I haven't had any previous problems – or at least nothing that has caused me to seek help – she asks me when I started to feel so low and anxious.

I don't feel low, I say. That's not it.

I am perched up high. Rosa's raw mouth, her precious hands – newly articulate – working over my chest, twisting the sensationless skin around my breasts as I feed her. I feel the vertigo of her falling even now.

OK, says Francesca. Not low. Could you explain to me what it is that you're feeling?

The air is ringing around me.

I want so much to speak. The force of what I've seen presses against my throat. It is intolerable not to say it – but I can't inflict the awful things that I've seen on this young, hopeful woman.

Try to. Trying to remember how to.

I can see that this is hard, Francesca says. I'm wondering if you might be experiencing. *Intrusive. Thoughts.* She is speaking very slowly as she says these words. These can take the form of disturbing images. Images of harm to your baby. These are very common, she says, after childbirth.

Francesca's kindness makes everything flood.

I've seen her falling, I say. I've seen Rosa ... I've seen my own hand—

I watch Francesca's response for signs of panic. Her face is distorted; her mouth turns down – in disgust or in pity, I don't know which.

She walks over to her desk and sends a document to her printer, which works slowly in the corner of the room. She could be alerting the authorities right now; she could be preparing the documents that are required to have me sectioned.

I'm printing a list, Francesca says, of common intrusive thoughts. These are responses from people who are not in clinical treatment; that is, these are thoughts that *'normal'* people – I'm speaking in inverted commas, right? – experience every day. I'd like you to read this list and tell me what you make of it.

Rosa has fallen asleep. I shrug my nipple back into my bra and begin to read:

Driving into oncoming traffic
Jumping in front of a car/train
Jumping off a high place
Stabbing a loved one
Slitting wrists/throat
Disgusting sex act
Eating contaminated food, or vomit, or excrement
Catching a fatal disease
Spreading a fatal disease
Accidentally leaving oven on
Leaving house unlocked, intruder inside

I read the list again. *Jumping off a high place. Stabbing a loved one.* I'm reeling; I must have misunderstood.

Did you say these were everyday thoughts? I ask Francesca.

Yes, Francesca says, everyone has thoughts like these. They

flicker in and out of our minds all the time. And then Francesca does something that stuns me: she writes down some of her own thoughts and reads them aloud to me:

I'll push my girlfriend and she'll hit her head on the pavement. I'll drive my car off a bridge in a moment of madness. I'll stab my girlfriend with a sharp kitchen knife when I'm cooking.

Incredible. That this composed woman can coexist with these intentions. That she can say this aloud, her voice steady, then look me straight in the eyes, her countenance warm and enquiring.

I wonder, Francesca says, if you know anything about a condition that's called obsessive-compulsive disorder?

Francesca tells me that normal, glitchy thoughts become alarming for people with OCD. That they experience passing cognitions as though they are premonitions or intentions, and that their anxiety escalates, making these thoughts more frequent. That they develop safety behaviours to try to protect themselves – rituals to ward off danger, some of which might be invisible, like counting.

I feel no connection to the letters that Francesca keeps repeating – O-C-D / O-C-D / O-C-D – but I am listening to her hungrily. And maybe there's something in what she is proposing, because the things that I've seen can't all be true. Rosa can't drown *and* choke *and* suffocate *and* scald *and* bleed out *and* fall to her death *and* be skinned alive. An infant can only die once.

Isobel asks me how the session went. I'm sitting with Rosa on the sofa back in the flat and I repeat Francesca's clean language of *intrusive thoughts*. I use the term *OCD* experimentally. I try to imagine that what I have seen is the result of anxiety, as Francesca told me. That my mind is suffering from a glitch in its processing, and I have been tagging my own thoughts incorrectly: as *<premonition>* rather than *<anxiety projection>*.

As I am doing this, talking to Isobel about the intrusive thoughts that apparently everyone has, I glance down at Rosa, feeding in my arms, and see her as a skinned rabbit – raw and naked at my breast – and my throat floods with nausea.

My story is splitting again. Like a heart, cross-sectioned: sliced in half then pried apart.

In one story of myself, I have seen the future; I feel it surging through my body still. What I have seen is rooted in my nerves and in the cords of my throat. It is in the song of the air. It is the deepest, darkest, most physical kind of knowledge. Clairvoyance. Mother's intuition.

On the other hand, I have a *disorder*. I have a problem with anxious thinking, which needs to be treated. Francesca is asking me to begin to live in a recovery narrative.

Imagine the most frightened you've ever been. Imagine sitting in a derelict mill in the dead of night in 1993 with your little sister and one of her friends, the light from a torch ghosting her face, the stink of pigeon shit in your nostrils, and someone's telling a scary story, something about a dog panting, blood pooling and drip drip dripping, something warm licking your hand in the dark, and suddenly there's a clang from the decommissioned machinery around you. Your heart swoops, the hair on your arms lifting, all three of you breathless, too scared even to scream, darting around in the darkness, falling over each other to get out, and away from that clang clang clanging—

Imagine someone telling you that what you feared in that moment was just a thought.

Your body knows your fears are irrefutable. They're bone-marrow knowledge. The Ripper. The Moors Murderers. Jimmy Savile. They were real and omnipresent in the Colne Valley. My body knew it.

No one can reason you out of your fears without gaslighting you.

And yet Francesca is asking me to go back into that mill and sit in the darkness. I must let my fears flood me, to prove to myself that they have no premonitory power.

We make a list of the things that could happen to Rosa that scare me the most. I must sit with these thoughts, for longer and longer, until my anxiety recedes.

Exposure therapy:

I stand at the top of a staircase with Francesca next to me, and I imagine hurling Rosa down to the ground floor. I listen to the awful wet smack of Rosa's head on the tiles.

I boil a kettle in the tiny kitchen at the old chapel with Rosa in my arms as the steam rises around us.

I lay out knives and scissors on the kitchen worktop.

I strike a match in proximity to my baby.

I rasp a lighter into flame.

The baby cries and cries, all hours of the day and night. We haven't seen the mother in weeks. In the secret of that flat, I hear the wet fizz of the baby's flesh.

Francesca keeps firmly and calmly to her line: I must allow my fears to flood. That is how I will learn to understand that they are only thoughts and that they cannot possess me.

I meet with Francesca twice a week. When I tell her about my night-times since the medication – the dark corridor down which I hurtle in my mind with Rosa, always towards the stairwell, my breathing ragged, my vision blurred, everything accelerating, as I watch my baby falling – Francesca says: That sounds like a panic attack, Grace. It's very common.

She asks me if I have any questions about my treatment plan.

Yes, I say. How long before these ... *thoughts* go away? What do I have to do to make them go away as soon as possible?

I am hoping that Francesca might answer my first question in hours, or perhaps even minutes, rather than days or weeks.

It's not always helpful, Francesca says, to focus on a timescale.

It is a bright blue day and Francesca and I stand on Lendal Bridge above the River Ouse. The balustrade on Lendal Bridge is highly decorated: the ironwork is studded with white roses and the crossed keys of the diocese of York and the red lions of England. The bridge was built in 1863 in the Gothic style and a central section bears an ornate interlocking set of initials painted in gold: V&A. Victoria and Albert.

I concentrate on these details so that I don't have to look at the water.

But I *must* look.

Flooding. This is the process by which I will learn to tolerate my fears. I must not shut anything out: no blocking, no distracting myself, no counting or looking for pairs of magpies to save me. Let all the worst thoughts flood in.

The water barely seems to be moving today. The cruise boats, tethered to the jetty, are almost too still. But this water is deceptive. The currents here are deep and strong, even when the river looks sedate. The Aire, the Wharfe, the Swale and the Nidd all converge in the Ouse. The rain that falls on the Pennines, the rain that falls in the Dales and the North Yorkshire Moors, pours into this river. Days after downpours in distant Yorkshire valleys, the Ouse will flood.

I watch as my hands lift Rosa out of her pram, my trembling hands holding her above the water. I hear the cold splash of my baby entering the river.

The water closes over Rosa. And then she disappears from my sight.

There is a body of water not far from York called the Strid. It is highly picturesque. The Strid is part of the River Wharfe, which runs close to Bolton Abbey, through Strid Wood – an ancient forest that is home to sessile oaks and roe deer, that is dappled in bluebells in the springtime and then wild garlic. At the heart of this woodland, the river narrows suddenly. There are large, mossy rocks at either side, and the distance across the river is only *a stride*. Stride the Strid. Reviews online rate the Strid a five-star experience: *A lovely place for a stroll / Great for a family walk with children and the dog*. You might take selfies next to the bluebells and the burbling Wharfe and finish your walk along the river with scones at the Strid Wood Tea Rooms.

The Strid – this delicate scene of English pastoral – is among the most dangerous stretches of water in the world. It takes its name from the Anglo-Saxon *stryth*, or strife; or from that temptation of crossing in a *stride*. Where the river narrows to a delicate-looking stream at the heart of the wood, the water is forced downwards with enormous pressure. All the water that has coursed here from the Yorkshire Dales, through Oughtershaw and Kettlewell and Coniston, all the water that has drained into the Wharfe from sinkholes on Yockenthwaite Moor and Horse Head Moor, all the water that has gushed in from Hagg Gill and Hush Gutter and Robin Hood's Beck, all of it is driven below ground at the Strid.

The rushing water has worn the soft, underground rock away and the banks at Strid Wood are undercut by a deep vertical ravine. The river changes course here: it moves downwards. As a result, the Strid is prone to dramatic flooding: after heavy rain, when the streams surging down from the Dales are forced through this narrow passage, the water can rise at the surface by five foot in under a minute.

No one who enters the Strid has ever survived it.

The Strid was one of my childhood fears. On special occasions, Dad would take me and Isobel and our nan to Bolton Abbey, and he'd point to the warning signs. There was a well-publicised case in the '90s: a couple on their honeymoon had been swallowed when the Strid suddenly flooded. A witness saw the man's body briefly bob to the surface, before it was sucked under and into the ravine again. Both bodies were eventually retrieved downstream, snagged on riverbeds miles apart. The honeymooners became an urban legend. Teenagers dared each other to cross the Strid.

When we visited, I often imagined falling into the Strid – or rather, I imagined jumping in. A wild kind of vertigo. Worse, I sometimes imagined I might push Isobel in. I made myself keep well back from the edge.

These memories flood me as I stand on Lendal Bridge.

The ghost of a face glimpsed beneath the surface of the water. They spend weeks searching this river for the bodies of adults. A baby's body might not cohere for long enough to ever be recovered.

I think I'm going to vomit or pass out.

Francesca instructs me to take Rosa from her pram and hold her.

I shake my head, but she is implacable.

I do as I'm told. I weep as I hold her against my chest, my heart beating against her heart. I can't look at her directly then, at her soft and expectant face. Her legs are wiggling with excitement. She knows nothing of what I can see. I press my mouth against her woollen hat.

I think of that woman who entered the water from Lendal Bridge, and the eerie silence that followed. The collective intake of breath. Someone from below, working on one of the cruise boats, shouting, *Here, here,* as he stood at the side of the boat and moved a pole through the water. Of the man walking past me and Tariq, saying, *What are you waiting for? It's a body they're looking for now you know. You waiting to see a body?*

But there was nothing to see by then. Only the dark, reflective surface of the Ouse.

Tourists continue to stroll across the bridge. What must they think of this woman standing with her baby in her arms, her face scored with tears as she stares at the water?

They might think of the bunches of flowers that are tied to the balustrade every so often, and that I am grieving one of the desperate souls who entered the water.

And I am in mourning. I am in mourning for my baby's future. But I have no right to this grief. I have to learn to tolerate this too: my disgust at my own unearned sorrow.

My thoughts begin to slow a little.

There, Francesca says. There you go. Well done. She squeezes my arm. Let's stay a little while longer, she says.

I sobel's departure is abrupt. I suppose that she might have planned it that way for my benefit. Rip the plaster off good and quick. But when she makes the announcement, I feel a sting of abandonment – the same sting I felt the morning after Rosa's birth, when the midwife came to evict me from the maternity bed.

Right, Isobel says, as I'm making toast. I'm off back to the Hud today.

Today, I say. Are you for real?

Don't be like that, Isobel says. I know you think I've got nothing going on, but I actually do. There's some work coming up at the Packhorse that I could do with taking. Also, my nails really fucking need attention and it's three times the price in York. And anyway, you're good, Grace. You are. I've watched you with this baby, day and night, and you're doing good. You don't need me here. The medication has settled down now, hasn't it?

The nights have softened, that is true. The medication has begun to blunt the edges of my hallway panic.

No need to come to the train station, Isobel says to me. I'll walk you to your class, and then I'll be off. Is it Rhyme Time today?

Isobel has made me plan a regime of mum and baby focused

activities. *Come on, Grace*, she said to me. *You love this shit! Let's find all the baby groups in York where you can go to meet other mad mothers. Ha!* I discovered the secret industry of morning groups. The breastfeeding support group recommended by the midwife, which meets on Thursdays. Music classes, story times, a baby sensory group, a gentle parenting circle, a mother and baby yoga class. I now have a plan to do something every day that forces me to spend time with other adults.

When I first attended a mother and baby group, I didn't talk about what I had seen – not about the ancient dead mothers of York, and not about my feeling that I might recently have met the Devil during my night-time feeding sessions. I could tell that these were not the best gambits with which to engage other new mothers. I am learning that the acceptable vocabulary of these gatherings is: sleep patterns; feeding patterns; birth trauma (indirect references only); self-care and the difficulty thereof; incontinence (physical not emotional); the unbearable proximity or uninterest of in-laws; the precociousness or developmental barriers of our infants. At these groups, I am surrounded by gorgeous, bright-eyed, brightly dressed little creatures who are attended by mothers who look grey with exhaustion. I try to assemble normal conversation. I try to share the everyday concerns of the other parents. This is not so much fakery as hope: that I'll be able to root myself in their concerns too, that I'll be able to make myself worry about teething and speech development, instead of the total annihilation of my baby.

I have attended appointments with a herbalist and a reflexologist and an acupuncturist too. *And how was the birth?* each of them asked me, heads inclined, awaiting the disclosure of a terrible rupture. All these activities are an expensive act of faith. I am haemorrhaging money, but it feels good to be planning these things.

All right then, I say to Isobel. Walk with me to Rhyme Time and we'll see you off.

Keep pushing the pram. Isobel leaving and my stomach lurching downwards. A seagull wheeling high in the sky above us. Not falling. No auguries of falling. Not today.

When Ryan arrives home I ask how his day's been.

Yeah, knackering, he says. Who knew there were so many dickheads who come to York for coffee. Dickheads from America. And dickheads from Germany. And even dickheads from Leeds. And you know what? They don't even like coffee. The stuff we do is proper nice, ethically sourced, roasted on-site, and these dickheads want vanilla syrup and three sugars and cinnamon sprinkles. Of course it doesn't taste any good, mate. Just buy a fucking milkshake round the corner if that's what you want. Fucking hell, I really need to get some gigs going again. Sorry, he says. What about you? How's your day been?

I tell him Isobel's gone.

I can see him wavering between relief and worry. You OK with that? he says.

Yeah, I say. It was a bit of a shock, but it's OK.

You seem like you're doing good, he says, tentatively. I'm proud of you, doing the treatment and that. Does that sound patronising? I don't always know . . . the best way to talk to you about this stuff.

I look at Ryan for the first time in a while. He's young enough that his tiredness makes him more intensely fit; his jaw and his cheekbones are more pronounced; he looks like he's really been *through it*. I know he must miss his friends and his life on the boat. I know he's been worried about me: when I told him about the medication and that I was suffering with 'intrusive thoughts' he did a good job of keeping a poker face and of saying the right things – but I caught his Adam's apple bobbing like it did when I first told him I was pregnant, as though he might be stopping himself from vomiting.

No, I say. It doesn't sound patronising. I appreciate you ... trying to talk about it.

Why don't I take Rosa for a bit, he says. Let you have a half an hour to yourself?

I want very much to go and lie down, alone, in the bedroom. But also the evenings are when Rosa is fussiest. Sometimes, Ryan will get as far as putting Rosa in her pram for a walk, and then she frets and screams and can only be soothed by being milk-fed again. If I can't get to Rosa when she starts crying – if Ryan tries walking her around the flat to soothe her, or wants to try taking her out, for example – then I begin to enter a physical state like withdrawal. I'm restless, edgy; I fear I might become violent. I'll do anything to get to her. If her cries escalate, I sometimes find myself tearing her from Ryan's arms.

It's OK, I say. You know what she's like in the evenings.

Ryan sits next to me on the sofa while I feed Rosa. Then he goes and gets a beer. Then he starts up with the lighter, rasping it against his thumb.

Maybe, he says, not now, like, because I know Isobel's only just gone. But, maybe, sometime soon, I could try to get some gigs. Because ... it's not really like I'm helping much in the evenings, is it? I was thinking, just a couple of nights a week, if I can get something close by. Or maybe in Leeds. Or even some weekend busking.

I try to sound casual, though I can hear the air begin to ring around me. But not just yet, right?

Right, he says. Not just yet. But, maybe, soon?

O nce, you lived your life mostly in the daylight. You thought about daylight things. You spoke in the daylight with other adults. Trying to. Remember. How to.

I have been ignoring Tariq's messages since Rosa's birth, mostly fobbing him off with emoticons. He was all bants about it at first. *Why you ghosting me, babe? Do I mean nothing to you now you don't need your metadata fixing??* Then he switched tack: *I know newborns can be super intense. If you don't go a bit insane, you're not doing it right. But are you OK, Grace?* Then he returned, mercifully, to the bants: *Send baby pics! I promise to say she's pretty even if she looks like a pug. / STILL no reply, Grace?? You're giving me more grey hairs. / DO I NEED TO STAGE AN INTERVENTION???*

I arrange to meet Tariq in his lunch hour. When he steps off the bus in front of me, my main aim is not to cry. He'd be mortified. I'd have to resign out of shame.

So, Tariq says, as we fall into step together around the ring road. This baby's real then, I was beginning to wonder. Aw, Grace, she is pretty! I don't even have to pretend! Let's get coffee then.

I ask him about work, and how he's finding acting into my role.

When are you coming back? he says. I know it's sort of illegal for me to ask, but seriously, when are you coming back?

You're enjoying it that much?

Right, OK, now you've asked for it.

He tells me about supplier issues and system failures and difficult authors and how one member of our team has gone on long-term sick. Tariq was authorised to check his email in his absence and discovered a long, sexually explicit correspondence with someone claiming to be a seventeen-year-old girl in financial distress in Moldova, and now Tariq feels dirty and wants to write an anonymous note to the man's wife, who is presently caring for him after his stroke.

Tariq buys us coffee and sandwiches, and we sit on a bench at the edge of the ring road.

I have actually been thinking about work, I say. I'm totally skint now my maternity pay's gone down. Could you send some cases my way? I could use my keeping-in-touch days to do them and get some pay.

It's not just the money I'm after: I'm desperate for structured activity. I want to try to put information in order again; to ward off all this disorder.

Yeah, course I can, Tariq says. You can take a whole load of mine seeing as they never got any extra cover in for *my* case reports while I'm covering *yours*. I'm not saying that you – tiny, cute, innocent, little baby – have made my life a living hell. But . . .

Rosa starts to cry.

I'm going to have to feed her, I say. Are you going to freak out?

Grace, he says. I do have three children, you know. I have even, on at least a couple of occasions, changed a nappy.

I lift Rosa out of her pram. Tariq feeds me my sandwich while I nurse her.

See, he says, I still have my uses.

When Rosa has finished, he asks to hold her.

You don't think I came to see you, do you, Grace? he says. Where's the cuddle for Uncle Tariq, then?

I pass her across. Tariq handles her gracefully. He crosses his arms to make a hammock and swings her back and forth. Rosa is dimpling up.

She likes me! he says. Look, she really likes me!

Do not cry. Do not cry in front of Tariq.

So, how's it been with Ryan? Tariq asks me as we walk back towards the bus stop. Is he stepping up to fatherhood?

Yeah, I say. He adores Rosa. But I suppose there's not that much anyone can do while I'm still breastfeeding. He's working long hours, and he really needs to find some guitar work, or he's never going to get established here. He wants to start looking for evening gigs.

When you've been alone with the baby all day? Tariq says. Nah, mate. That's not on. You must be knackered. It sends you mad being with a baby all the time. I remember Michelle with our first. Crying when I got home from work with ... I don't know. Exhaustion? Relief? She'd lock herself in the bathroom and just tell me I had to take care of the baby. You need to make sure he's pulling his weight, Grace.

The thought of being locked on the other side of a door from Rosa is wonderful and agonising. Even the thought of her crying for me makes milk flush through my chest like panic.

He's doing his best, I say. It's me, not him, that's the problem. Ryan's given up a lot to be here.

Really, says Tariq, because it sounds to me like he's landed on his feet. No proper job, living on some squalid boat, and now he's fixed up here with you paying most of the rent. Watch out that you don't end up looking after two of them, Grace.

It's not like that, I say. You know what, he actually had a life he *enjoyed*. Doing work he wanted to do. Living in the way that he wanted to live. Imagine that?

I can't, says Tariq. Because grown-ups don't get to live that way. They have to take care of other people.

Tariq's wife, Michelle, fell pregnant when Tariq was still training to be a solicitor. He gave up his aspirations to practise law in favour of routine hours and a reliable starting salary with a legal publisher. Tariq had wanted to practise immigration law and represent asylum cases, and now he's covering a list of civil procedure texts and torts law: where there's blame, there's a claim.

Tariq's bus is pulling in.

Right, back to the grindstone, he says. You've got a right bobby-dazzler there, Grace. Honest. Not even a touch of the pugs.

Ta very much, I say.

Oh! he says. I nearly forgot. He hands me an envelope. Vouchers. You have to make a small human or be bereaved to get this amount from the stingy bastards we work with. Not sure which is worse. Spend them wisely.

A day of brightness, unspooling gently as Rosa wakes me with her babble-song. Remembering. How to. Think in the daylight. Think outside the tunnel of darkness.

York is a spill of raw green and white – hawthorn and horse chestnut flowers edge the river, dandelion clocks and nettles and daisies fill the verges. Rosa gathers all this into her ravenous eyes. Everything is brand new to her. She's mesmerised by the changing patterns of colour and light; the gluey smell of fresh growth; she's mesmerised by my face. When I lift her from the pram, she stares at me with deep, loving hunger – pushes her fingers into my mouth, then gums on my chin.

Rosa has begun to laugh; a hard little bleat of joy that surprises us both. Rosa loves surprises. When Ryan appears suddenly from behind his own hands, when he bounces her especially high, she hammers with this new laughter. Her movements around me have become kittenish. She hides, coyly, face pushed into my breasts, rubbing her eyes, rubbing her face against my skin. Then, a sudden burst of exuberance, hands hitting my collarbones, wild mewling. She'll try to cast herself off, away from me – arching backwards, kicking her feet against the floor, furious for movement.

Light begins to spill into our days together, but at night-time, when I wake in the quiet hours – those hours when your body is a sensitive device for danger – I still feel the lure of the staircase, and the night sky sings to me again.

I wake Ryan then. I tell him that I need him to stand next to me as I try to stay with my fears. And he comes with me, right out on to the landing, and he stands at my side in the middle of the night as I weep and watch Rosa spilling from my arms. He stays with me until my breath slows and my visions begin to thin. His arm is around my shoulders. It's OK, Grace, he says. You're OK.

I have always found it difficult to believe that I have a personality. I used to take quizzes in magazines and read horoscopes and fill in the Myers–Briggs questionnaire to try to discover if I had any defining characteristics. I was once at a party with a girl who claimed to read auras – she said she saw them around people in bright colours – and she went round a circle telling people their hue, and then when she got to me, she said: *That's funny. You don't seem to have an aura.* And I thought at the time: *Yeah, that's a sick burn, but also – fair enough.*

Francesca asks me to think about my personality, and the ways in which I have learned to cope with my fears. My disorder may have been triggered by Rosa's arrival, Francesca says, but it will have deep roots.

I tell Francesca that I don't have a personality; Isobel is the one with a personality.

Francesca laughs and asks what I remember from being small. What frightened me most when I was young?

So I begin:

I was born on the day that the last victim of the Yorkshire Ripper was discovered. I was born in the Colne Valley, into a seam of abandoned mills. I grew up in a house just ten miles, as the crow flies, from Saddleworth Moor, where children were buried in unmarked graves by the Moors Murderers. My childhood was a map marked with danger zones. Titanic Mills, filled with broken glass and pigeon shit, in which we were forbidden to play. The lanes and ginnels and car parks that ran behind old coal yards and pubs, in which we were forbidden to play. The secluded crescents of greenspace next to the canal where people dumped old sofas and chest freezers and cans of paint, in which we were forbidden to play. We were never, ever, to wander off the beaten track. We were never, ever to walk up towards Scapegoat Hill or Marsden Moor, we were never to go up to the moortop, to the forbidden and terribly beautiful places: Dovestones Edge and the Boggart Stones.

When we were small, we nurtured our fears together, Isobel and I. We created a constellation of fears to worship, and our dearest was that something would happen to our mother.

I was full of terror, when Mum disappeared.

How so? Francesca asks.

At bedtime, there was the terrible roar of the joyriders to contend with and my fear of the valley around me, alive with danger. We knew about domestics. *Where is Mum? What have you done to her?* I checked in the wardrobe and under our bunks. I adjusted the angle of our bedroom door, so that there would be a continuous crack of hallway light – a narrow enough slice of light that my sister could still sleep, but wide enough that I could keep a check on the dark shapes in the corners of our bedroom. I would spend a while before bed adjusting the curtains and checking that the plug sockets were switched off – and while neither of these activities was directly related to the probability of me and Isobel being murdered in our beds, it felt necessary to keep us safe.

I prayed too, though I had only a gruesome sense of Jesus from Sunday School visits with Nan – a picture in my mind of the crucifixion and of a millstone placed around a sinner's neck to drown them in the depths of the sea. But still, I prayed to the Dear Terrifying Lord Jesus, to keep me and Isobel and our mother safe from harm.

Francesca asks if I ever see my mother now.

Every so often, I say.

And has she met Rosa?

No, I say.

Why not?

Because, I say, she doesn't live close by. And she's no good at making plans. I'd have to get on a train with Rosa. And, I don't know. I don't know if it would ... upset her. Hurt her. To have to see us.

What would that look like, to hurt your mother, what would that feel like?

My mother, sobbing into our hair, wordless, racked with grief.

My mother, a ghost in the window of Storthes Hall, then disappearing into the earth.

Ryan brings pizzas home and we eat them straight out of the box while Rosa sleeps in her Moses basket. The melted cheese adheres to the cardboard and to our teeth. Ryan folds his slices of pizza into sandwiches and finishes them quickly – we've learned to eat rapidly, anticipating Rosa's interruptions.

When we've finished, we both stare at the Moses basket on the other side of the room.

Well, Ryan says. She's actually sleeping at the right time. A miracle.

I watch the basket. Rosa's stillness is more unnerving than her crying. I'll just check— I start to say, wanting to get closer to listen for Rosa's breathing.

Don't check anything! Ryan says. You know she'll wake up. Come and sit over here and I'll make you a cup of tea.

Ryan leads me to the sofa. He brings me tea and he cracks open another beer. Then he is sitting right next to me.

Ryan strokes my arm, slowly.

I can smell his body. Yeast. Sweat. Coffee.

You used to live in the world with other adults. You used to love the bodies of other adults – the tacky warmth, the salt of skin, the clean tang of sweat. Trying. Trying to remember. How you used to love Ryan's scent. That first time on the boat, you kissed and it was awkward in the small space. The water moved you back and forth and back and forth. When you woke, the dankness of river and damp wood, the vegetal smell of the boat's bathroom, the salt of Ryan's skin – all of it was rich and delicious to you.

But now his body next to me smells thickly masculine and alien. He smells like a threat – and not in a good way.

I have become adept at avoiding Ryan's touch, which he extends to me less and less frequently. When he gets home from work, he kisses me in a brotherly fashion, sometimes on the cheek, sometimes on the mouth. My doctor, in a recent check-up on the phone, asked me how I was healing and if I'd been ... *intimate* with my partner since the birth. Would I like to talk through contraceptive options? Because you certainly could become pregnant while breastfeeding, the idea that you couldn't was a myth, and the doctor said her third child was the living proof of that. No, we hadn't been *intimate* since the baby. We have shared a bed from necessity while Isobel was with us, but Ryan and I are still living in different worlds. He has remained in adult life; I have been down in the underworld of infants.

Ryan is still stroking my arm. Friction accumulating in my skin like the heat of a burn.

Queasy closeness of Ryan's scent.

My sensory apparatus has been re-tuned. Rosa's scent – the clean sweetness of her body, the milk curd of her breath, even the tang of her dense, warm nappies – are my new olfactory field. I can smell when Rosa has a fever even before I check her temperature; there is a tiny sulphurous shift in the scent of her breath. My senses are totally reoriented towards Rosa, and I can't make myself return from her.

I can't, I say to Ryan, lifting his hand away from my arm. I just— I can't. I'm sorry.

I wasn't, he says. I was only—

And then he gasps – a sudden inhale, as forceful and unexpected as his orgasm used to be to me. He folds one arm over his face.

I sit very still. Panic is rising like a laugh from my belly. I'm witnessing something he wouldn't want me to see, and my instinct is to turn away.

But that's cowardly. Ryan has witnessed me naked on all fours as the midwives dragged our baby out, disinterring her from inside me. He's stood beside me on the landing, when I was silent with fear. The least I can do is stay while he cries.

Sorry, he says, when the sobbing's subsided. His face is blotchy. I'm really not trying to guilt you or anything. It's just . . . fucking hard, isn't it.

O nce upon a time, you loved to put things in order. It felt possible to organise information, to code, to hierarchise, to edit. You worked through your cases with accuracy and speed, totally absorbed by them. Try. Trying to remember how.

While Rosa naps one afternoon, I attempt to open my email. And I can't remember my username. I've entered it instinctually almost every day for the best part of a decade, but now it's been wiped from my mind. I ring through to IT in London and explain the situation.

Once I'm into the system, there's a stream of unread emails, which is deeper than I care to scroll. I check on Rosa – she's still sleeping – then I find Tariq's link to my cases and I begin.

My first cases are from domestic criminal courts in the UK. I used to work on these when I first joined the company. I read through the style sheets, and the example files, and the hierarchy of content, to get my eye back in. The Criminal Court cases follow a clear hierarchy: at the top is *case type*, which needs to be correctly assigned to make it searchable online. The categories include: *assault and non-fatal offences* / *drug offences* / *extradition* / *firearms offences* / *inchoate offences* / *murder and manslaughter* / *sexual offences* / *terrorism*.

These are simply content categories. There is no need to panic at a content category label. There is no need for my blood to run cold.

I open the raw text of the first case.

It's straightforward to categorise: a <*drug offence*>. I list <*The facts of the case*>. I standardise paragraphs and capitalisation and the style of dates. I amend measurement style too, so:

650 GBP in cash about her person, hidden in her bra

becomes

£650 in cash about her person, hidden in her bra.

And then:

fifteen grams of crack cocaine and around twenty-five grams of heroin

becomes

15g of crack cocaine and around 25g of heroin.

And then I make a fatal error – I start actually reading the content:

*The appellant had previously been a victim of sex trafficking …
The appellant was paid in drugs and not cash for her involvement …
The appellant had been in custody for nine months by the time of her sentencing.*

Miss Barnes, on behalf of the appellant, said that the appellant was hopelessly addicted to the drugs that she was supplying. The appellant had never been to prison before …

The failure to follow a lenient course does not give rise to grounds for appeal.

Appeal dismissed.

I'm picturing Isobel in the dock. Isobel in a cell, shivering in withdrawal. Isobel having the shit kicked out of her in the showers: pig's daughter; filthy scum.

It has taken me twenty minutes and I haven't even proofread the case.

I slam my laptop shut.

Then I open it again.

It will take a while, that's all. I have to learn again how to skim-read. I did this for years: skimming the surface of these documents without falling into them. Remember. How to. I just need to get back into the rhythm.

The second case is a <*road traffic offence*>. Keywords: *Dangerous driving; Domestic burglary; Disqualification from driving; Guilty pleas; Suspended leniency.* I amend it quickly, parse it, submit it.

The third case is a total fucking abyssal nightmare.

A number of witnesses noticed abrasions and cuts to the girl's body.

Social workers were told the injuries were self-inflicted.

The appellant said that the girl threw herself against hard objects and radiators.

... subdural bleeding ... signs of bleeding in the retina of each eye, indicative of shaking or impact ...

I stop reading.

I breathe deeply, as Francesca has taught me. I try to let my fears flood me.

I see the girl being shaken.

I look at Rosa, still asleep in her basket beside me. Breathe through it. Try to tolerate it.

I return to the case again, though the air is singing around me.

Related case ... manslaughter of a four-month-old ... the child would not stop crying ... apart from the occasion when he had shaken the child, the appellant had been a loving father ...

Rosa's sleeping face, soft as a mushroom; blood filling the delicate retinas behind her eyes.

The rasp of a lighter. That poor baby, crying through the day and night – then, at last, lapsing into silence.

Unparsable. Un-fucking-parsable content.

I used to be able to gloss this material, to cauterise content with metadata tags, hardly giving a second thought to a baby's bleeding retina; to a child's body raw with burns. And that was when my mind was supposedly orderly.

Francesca tells me that things get worse before they get better. New parents, she tells me, are often bombarded with thoughts of harm – of physical harm and emotional harm and the worst and most disgusting forms of sexual harm that they might commit against their own children. Some parents that Francesca has worked with had to stop touching their children entirely.

Intrusive thoughts, she tells me, cluster around the very things that you care most about. If you are devout, for example, you might fixate on the possibility of committing accidental sin. If you are anxious about money, you might fear that you will gamble any gain away or set fire to your own savings. If you want to do right by others, you might obsess about mistakes you've made that have damaged them. And if you want to care for someone vulnerable, if you deeply want to love and protect them, you might find that you think constantly of committing violence against them.

The technical term for this should be, I suggest, *a total fucker*.

I learn more about obsessive compulsive disorder. I google while I'm feeding Rosa and read everything I can find.

Long before the diagnostic term OCD was in use, the term *scrupulosity* was used to describe something similar, from the Latin, *scrupulum*, meaning a sharp stone. Scrupulosity as an instrument of torture against the scrupulous soul. There's a long religious history of scrupulosity – centuries and centuries of people suffering from an obsessional fear of committing sin:

A medieval German theologian, Johanne Nider, describes the case of the scrupulous nun, Kunegond of Nuremburg, who lived in terror of her own mortal sin. She engaged in frequent and excessive fasts and her confessors feared for her sanity and her life. John Bunyan, author of *The Pilgrim's Progress*, was *most distressed with blasphemies; if I have been hearing the Word, then uncleanness, blasphemies and despair would hold me as captive there; if I have been reading, then, sometimes, I had sudden thoughts to question all I read; sometimes, again, my mind would be so strangely snatched away, and possessed.*

I discover historical examples of 'safety behaviours', of counting and chanting and ritualised movements:

Dr Samuel Johnson, originator of the first English dictionary, would avoid stepping on cracks between paving stones. You'll break your mother's back. He counted the steps on staircases that he ascended. When walking, he was compelled to touch each post that he passed. He performed ritualised movements – a whirl, a twist, a gesture of the hand – before crossing a threshold.

Nikola Tesla, the electrical engineer and physicist who developed alternating current, became preoccupied with the number three. He swam thirty-three laps each day. He circled a block three times before entering a building. He counted as he chewed each mouthful of food.

Charles Darwin was haunted by the horrid spectacle of his children becoming ill. He tried to eradicate these thoughts by closing his eyes in a particular, ritualised way. He repeated a mantra: *I have worked as hard as I could, and no man can do more than this. I have worked as hard as I could, and no man can do more than this.*

These eminent male sufferers must be the tip of a deep iceberg. There is so much suffering of which there is no record. Centuries of mothers fearing for their infants. Centuries of mothers who thought that the Devil was calling them to put their babies on the fire, who thought themselves responsible for miscarriage and still-birth and infant mortality because of their thoughts. Who thought themselves witches. Who swaddled their newborns and left them on church steps or inside rabbit warrens or in phone boxes or at park gates, because they wanted their babies to be safe from harm. Because they wanted their babies to be safe from them.

Fasting was used to try to eradicate sinful thoughts. Bloodletting was used to try to relieve sinful thoughts. Self-harm and alcohol and narcotics and compulsive use of mobile phones and abandonment of your children and suicide are used to attempt to relieve bad thoughts. That sharp stone of scrupulosity dig dig digging away at our bodies and souls for centuries now.

Keep going, Francesca tells me. Keep letting your fears flood in. Keep going, Grace.

Grace, meaning *favour towards the unworthy*. Grace, meaning *mercy – for all have sinned and fall short*. Every one of us, falling.

Francesca encourages me to remember times when my fears haven't come true.

When I first visited London for work, for instance, I was astonished by the proximity of the platform to the Tube line and the disorderly bustle of it, with crowds edging you ever closer to the track. The sound of the train echoed through the tunnel towards me, and I felt a momentary vertigo, a horrible speeding sensation that made me fear I was about to throw myself in front of the train. I'd shaken it off, that feeling, but I was relieved that I didn't have to use the Tube too often.

And a few years ago, I went to stay in a hotel in Brighton with a man I was seeing. Our room was so high up that we could look out to sea and the gulls rode the thermals around us. We were drinking on the terrace, laughing and trading stories and knocking back something cold and delicious. And then I caught a glimpse of a gull swooping suddenly – and I saw myself run to the edge of the balcony and hurl myself over.

I didn't think I could sleep in that room after that awful rush of vertigo towards the edge, though the man was hot as fuck and had planned a long weekend of champagne and oysters and clean lines of coke for us. I briefly thought about trying to lose him – I could just go to the loo and never return and get the train back home – but I worked with him. He was a well-known human-rights lawyer who wrote for my publisher. I couldn't just disappear.

I was menaced by the view from the window that first night and I found ways for us to stay out as late as possible. But we were there for three nights, and by the end of the trip I'd pretty much forgotten about the drop from the room.

There, Francesca says when I tell her all this. Your mother wasn't buried under the patio. Your sister didn't overdose. You imagined yourself falling off that balcony, but it wasn't a premonition. It didn't happen. And when you realised that, the thought didn't bother you any more.

I begin to sleep again – for longer than twenty minutes at a time. Some nights, I sleep for a whole three-hour stretch, and my thoughts are soft as dreams when I wake. I let Rosa sleep next to me in the bed. We arrange everything to be as safe as possible. We keep the bedroom cool. We position blankets and pillows away from Rosa and check that the mattress is firm enough. I keep a list in my head now of the things that have helped to save my life – my sister; my kind GP; sertraline; Francesca, who I once thought too young and hopeful to be of any help – and now this. This blessed possibility of sleeping next to my baby.

Some mornings, Rosa wakes me as she snuffles for milk.

Dawn. Rosa's eyes glittering bright, her mouth seeking me. Rosa latches on and then looks hungrily at me, drinking me in, drinking in the world around us.

I have to look away from her then, because the greedy, boundless love of the world in Rosa's eyes, her incommensurate aliveness, is still hard to bear.

But sometimes, I am able to look at her in return. I kiss Rosa's head and breathe in her warm, yeasty scalp. Yes, baby. Yes, Rosa. Here we both are.

Rosa is six months old and has reached the twenty-fifth percentile for weight. She is changing all the time, her expressions shifting day by day. Some mornings, when she wakes, I can see that something has changed overnight.

She's had a software upgrade again, Ryan says, and he kisses her over and over.

Rosa laughs often, in those hard little staccato bleats of joy. She hides her face in my breasts after laughing, as though overwhelmed by the feeling or the sound from her own throat.

She has a special way of giving me a kiss: she leans into my face and then gums hard on my chin.

When Rosa feeds now, she sweeps her fingertips along my skin – along my arms and chest, seeming to want to learn my texture. It is like being explored by an enquiring alien.

The throb in my body when I feed her is gentler, though I still feel the draw of her hunger working on me, her needs like the tidal pull of the moon.

She tries to recreate the music of conversation: she babbles in long, tuneful patterns – la da da da da la la la, ma ma ma ma, da da da, ow wow ow wow bow wow wow, row row row, uh-ooh uh-ooh uh-ooh uh-ooh – her song of accidents, which will make it impossible for us to remember her first words, when they come, because they will emerge and recede, emerge and recede, back and forth in this music.

I am beginning to believe in the possibility of Rosa's life. That she might not be extinguished in the blink of an eye. I buy clothes for her in the next size up. I pack these little outfits away in drawers for her to grow into, and I try not to give credence to the flutter of panic I feel – for surely I am tempting fate – as I fold them away.

A Friday night. Full flush of summer. Ryan arrives home from work, excited and agitated. He's been given a trial gig at the Greek restaurant in town. He spends a few minutes playing with Rosa – singing to her, copying her sounds, rolling on the floor with her – so that I can make myself something to eat with the use of both of my hands. Then he gets ready to go out. He puts on a shirt. His hair has grown long and he sweeps it up into a bun. *Grace, have you seen my sheet music? Does my hair look shit? Do I look like a hipster wanker?* And then he's out the door with his guitar and amp. He comes home late – drunk and happy – whispers into the bedroom: It went well! They liked it!

Ryan is offered a regular Friday night spot.

I can see that he is afraid of what I might say – and I know that Ryan's life must often have felt like a dark corridor since Rosa's birth too.

I tell him it will be OK. I learn to tolerate my Friday evenings alone with the baby. The tunnel of the hallway, the drop of the staircase beyond it. I no longer try to shut them out and I travel down them in my mind less frequently now. I will not avoid being alone with Rosa. I will not avoid being alone with Rosa at night. I will not avoid boiling the kettle or opening the bathroom cupboards or cutting an onion with a sharp knife. I make myself do these tiny, terrible things, and little by little, they are becoming less terrible.

One night, Ryan is playing with Rosa on the rug before getting changed for his gig and suggests that Rosa and I come down to the restaurant to watch him.

Tomaso is always saying you should come down, he says. He'd make a right fuss of you both.

She needs her bath, I say. And you know how she can be before bed.

Maybe she'd be less fretful outside, Ryan says.

But what if she doesn't sleep, I say. What if she bawls the restaurant down. What if she needs to feed for hours. I can't, I say.

All right, he says. It's up to you. But look at that sky. Ryan nods towards the window.

The tree outside the flat is in full leaf, the sky behind it radiant blue.

Let me know, he says, if you change your mind.

I give Rosa her bath. I warm the baby cream in my hands and smooth it on to Rosa's skin, making myself touch all the tender places where the blood rises close to the surface. The backs of Rosa's knees, her soft wrists, the nape of her neck. Rosa burbles as I do this and rolls from side to side.

Can I do it? Can I put Rosa into the pram instead of the Moses basket and leave the flat at night-time? The thought of it is total panic. I have no pattern for how to manage her disorganised needs in this new scenario where there will be so many unpredictable hazards.

Screaming baby, milk leaking, my throat – I feel it in my throat, a knot of panic there, the hardness of a swallowed cry, Rosa thrashing into table cutlery and wine glasses, scalding hot coffee, my breasts throbbing with milk, nipple escape, serrated bread knife, Rosa's nappy leaking, baby sodden and screaming, screaming on a filthy toilet floor, Rosa's head against floor tiles, subdural bleeding, her soft spot, throbbing me all the way to prison. You pig's daughter. You agent of infanticide.

Peak anxiety. And then . . . slowly, my throat softens.

Rosa is still burbling away, catching her own feet in both hands, and the world is coming back into focus: here and now on the bathroom floor, Rosa with one foot in her mouth, drooling with the satisfaction of chewing it.

I dress her in her sleepsuit. I pack a bag with nappies and wipes and spare clothes and a teething toy and hand sanitiser and bread sticks. Then I put on lipstick, the most garish pink I can find. I message Ryan: *Is it still OK if I come down to the restaurant tonight? Xx*

I haven't been outside at night-time since Rosa was born – since last December when York was winter bare and lit by Christmas decorations. I step out into the evening, pushing the pram ahead of me, and it is like wading into the ocean, the warm blue extending all around me.

I walk along the ring road, through the flats at Hunstanton. The River Foss is a dark curve beside a demolition site, foxgloves and nettle flowers thickening at the bankside. Birds fly overhead. Music and Netflix drifting from open windows in the new student blocks. A teenage couple kicking the wall outside the sexual health clinic, dumb with desire.

Inside the city walls, crowds in pubs spill out on to the cobbled streets. Clusters of libidinous, shrieking, laughing strangers. A group of girls hard out on the lash, stumbling past me and into one another, yanking up their tops, mobbing a busker on the street up ahead and screaming along with the song.

Something strange and wonderful is happening as I watch the city's dark animation. It has to do with my depth perception: the world is zooming away from me – a careering out-there-ness of everything that isn't the baby. Pigeons are flocking in a gutter. A man urinates behind a bin. A maple tree extends itself into the blue. The air tastes of petrol and ozone, of the atmosphere that spreads from down here on Petergate all the way up to the furthest reaches of the sky. I remember reading about a symbolic marker that designates where the Earth's atmosphere ends and space begins, and it's called the Kármán line. Space officially begins sixty-two miles above our heads; space is closer to me than Manchester!

The restaurant manager, Tomaso, seats me and Rosa at a table on the pavement. He brings me bread and calamari and fizzy water and a board full of delicacies: peppers glossed with oil, sour cheese, capers the size of grapes. I can hear Ryan playing inside.

You need to eat, Tomaso says, when you're looking after a baby. You ask for anything that you want, and it's on the house!

Tomaso peers into the pram. Rosa is awake, her eyes wide and hungry for the sky.

Ah! Tomaso says. Beautiful!

Rosa kicks her legs hard and babbles.

Ha! Tomaso says. She really wants some conversation over dinner!

He shows me photographs of his two children on his phone.

Anything you want, he says, you just call for me. I'll tell Ryan he can take his break soon.

Rosa is burbling a little querulously now, her sounds rising towards distress. I lift her out of her pram and attempt to eat one-handed, but she squirms in my arms.

You must be Grace, a young waiter says. Ryan told me you might be coming down. Can I help? I could walk the baby while you eat.

He lifts Rosa out of my arms and begins to sway back and forth with her. He moves like a practised infant soother. Rosa is silent, staring at his face as he hums to her.

I don't want to alarm you, Grace, Ryan says, appearing next to me. But you seem to be missing a baby.

He looks shyly at me and then away again: diffident, like that first evening at the Christmas party.

He sits down next to me, scoops up some cheese, and we watch the man waltzing with our baby in his arms.

That's Christos, Ryan says. He's a good one. I think he's got, like, eight brothers and sisters back at home.

Rosa begins to bleat. I am beyond her line of sight, and I feel a little palpitation of my own separation anxiety. Christos dances in closer to us.

Ah, he says, my winning streak might be coming to an end.

It was a good run, I say, reaching for Rosa. Thank you.

My pleasure, he says. Now I have to go back to dirty dishes!

I pull down the shoulder of my top and let Rosa root for my breast. The release is fierce and sweet. I often feel a surge of light-headedness, almost like a swoon, when the baby first latches on now – and then her feeding becomes sensationless.

I'm glad you came down, Ryan says. Really glad. We could do more of this, you know. Come out in the evenings. Make the most of the summer's dog days.

Yeah, I say. Maybe.

Right, he says. I'd better get back to it. Ask for the honey pie for afters. It's lush. See you back at home?

Yeah, see you later on, I say. We might be asleep. Hopefully we'll be asleep.

Yeah, he says, I'll look in and sleep on the couch if you're settled. Love you, he says, leaning in and kissing Rosa on the back of her head.

I don't know if his words are meant for me or the baby. Me *and* the baby? Babymother. Grace-and-child.

I listen to the music again. I recognise elements of the piece from Ryan's practice at home: cheerful, jazzy chords, with something more discordant picked out above. I barely know Ryan, still. He mumbles *love you* some mornings as he leaves, but we've never made a declaration to one another, never gasped, *I love you, I love you*, in the throes of passion, never held one another, nose to nose, whispering tender, implausible promises. We've bypassed the ecstatic for survival mode. In the early days, Ryan was in the background of my demented infatuation with Rosa. He is coming back into focus now, along with the rest of the world. Ryan has been there this whole time, quietly learning how to love Rosa too. Ryan has been beside me at the top of the staircase at the dead of night. I don't know how the three of us will constellate, re-constellate, find our places around one another. But I know he'll always be there. Ryan. Babyfather. Constant friend.

*

Rosa falls asleep as I walk back towards our flat, her cheeks flushed, the fluff of her hair stuck to her head. My baby is sleeping soundly. Blissfully. But that roll of her eyes just before she goes under still makes me think of an aneurism. Is that deep flushed dampness of her cheeks the start of a fever? I can never know what the next turn of my baby's breath will bring; this world is too wild and vast and alien for us to know what will come next.

I am living in a recovery narrative. Most of the time. I have a new Content Management System for my thoughts and I tag aberrant images as 'anxiety', so that they can then be filed away correctly. But I have my own theories too. Analogies proliferate in my mind, post-hoc philosophies that cause glitches in the new filing system.

For instance:

Late summer. The time of the year when everything else gives up in the heat and the wasps move in. I walk with Rosa into town, the air close around us. I buy myself an ice cream from the good Italian place on Goodramgate, and when the ice cream begins to melt, I give some to Rosa to drink from the tub like milkshake. She screws her hands into fists and hammers them on my chest in excitement.

There is a yellow tinge to the clouds above us. Warm, leaking, amniotic sky.

By the time we are back at the city walls, fat drops of rain have begun to fall. Then there is a roll of thunder. I up my pace.

Lightning forks in the sky over the River Foss. A luminous tree shooting down roots.

I begin to run with the pram.

What is the rule again? To avoid tall things when there's lightning, or to shelter under them because they're higher than you?

For the millionth time I ask myself: How can I be trusted to care for a baby when I don't understand the basics of life and I can't even remember what you're supposed to do in a thunderstorm?

Lightning flashes over Sainsbury's. Lightning flashes over the secret Jewish burial ground.

A bolt from the blue. Someone's got to be the one in a million. I read recently that a woman and her toddler had been walking under scaffolding in the centre of York when a car hit one of the supports and the scaffolding fell. The child had been badly injured. The sky does sometimes fall. Chicken Licken gets an unfair press.

I run towards the flat. Rain saturates my hair and begins to darken the fabric of Rosa's pram.

Once I'm safely inside, I strip Rosa, get her into clean, dry clothes, and I google what to do when there's lightning. I discover that lightning can strike up to ten miles away from the centre of a storm. If the count between thunder and lightning is less than thirty seconds, then there is a threat of being struck. If you are inside, you should avoid using running water in case electricity hits the metal plumbing. If you are outside, you should crouch to make yourself as small as possible.

I discover that just before lightning strikes, you can feel the charge around you. The air will crackle with static. Your fingertips will tingle and the hair on your arms will stand on end. When lightning strikes, ions move up through the earth as well as down from above. Objects in close proximity to you may begin to hum – a metal gate, or a car on the street – and the humming will get louder as the lightning nears. The taste of metal will fill your mouth. This means that the electrical charge has already begun to enter your body. You should be running by now, away from the open sky, as fast as you can.

That's just it, I think. That's what I've been feeling. Caring for a baby is like being in the midst of an electrical storm. Loving an infant is like lightning entering your body ahead of the strike.

For instance:

I remember how I lived before Rosa, the way I could edit my cases without reading them, gliding over the details; the way my personal life ricocheted between acute sensitivity and total recklessness.

Perhaps the pain of being alive was slow to emerge for me. It bloomed after giving birth. It's like when you burn your fingertips on a hot tin, and you feel nothing at first. I'm fine! you say. I can hardly feel it! But the burn grows slowly, steadily, until, days later, all you can feel is the pulse of that pain in your fingertips.

Loving an infant is deferred effect.

For instance:

I listen to a podcast about scurvy. I'm listening to lots of programmes now, trying to expand my thoughts as I feed Rosa and settle her at night. I discover that in severe cases of scurvy, the body cannot heal itself. Vitamin C is needed to make collagen, which supports the structure of blood vessels, as well as the production of scar tissue. For centuries, sailors lost their teeth, blood pooling in their mouths and under the skin, blood leaking into their internal organs, their bodies reeking of rot. And here is the kicker: in the final stages of scurvy, injuries that healed long ago, that were hidden by collagen, begin to appear again. Bones re-break. Old wounds split back apart.

And then I think: Oh, that's it. Having a baby forces you to move backwards through your own injuries; it dissolves your superficial healing.

Loving an infant is morbid regression.

For instance:

When Rosa begins to crawl, I scan our living room for small, ingestible objects, tiny things which could be lethal, and I then I think: Perhaps this problem is more to do with scale than anything else. The dimension and proportion of things has gone awry.

A popcorn kernel can end your baby's life. Rosa was born with a stomach the size of a grape, and yet her hunger had overwhelmed me.

When you have a baby, all your attention, your every concern, is suddenly condensed on to your baby's body – system glitch / meningitis / flood warning / lightning strike / climate crisis / forty-nine burns in a toddler's sweet flesh – all of this, whole massive load of world, pressurised on to your baby's body.

It's like the Strid then: all that force in too small a channel has to move downwards.

Loving an infant is vortex dynamics.

For instance:

This isn't my problem! The problem is endemic to the organisation of parenthood. To the privatisation of the task of parenting and to the nuclear family. To the belief that the right product, the right schedule, the right approach to feeding and weaning, the right sleep training, the right parenting philosophy, will solve the problems of being alive.

I know from devising workflows and robust systems that nothing important should be totally dependent on one person. You should never only be one person deep.

But mothers are told they must protect their infants from *everything* – from childhood illnesses and secondary smoke inhalation and malnutrition and disordered eating and racial injustice and depression and poverty – mothers are charged with somehow keeping their children safe from all the failings of the world, and how can one person possibly do that?

Loving an infant is a political tragedy.

For instance:

A line from *Julius Caesar*, which I must have memorised for my university exams, visits me again:

Cowards die many times before their deaths, / The valiant never taste of death but once.

Come off it, Caesar. Caesar speaks this line just before he's stabbed to death. Caesar is accusing his wife, Calpurnia, of cowardice, of giving too much credence to portents – to comets, and thunder and lightning, to reports of graves yawning and yielding up their dead. Calpurnia sees Caesar's death everywhere – she hears the ghostly sounds of battle in the streets, of dying men groaning – and she has to find a way to endure the images of his suffering all around her. She sees blood drizzle from the sky. She hears the crying of soldiers. Calpurnia is not afraid for herself;

she thinks not of her own death. She trembles because she loves another – she cries out in her sleep: *They murther Caesar*!

Loving an infant and seeing her suffering is an act of valour.

For instance:

Moments of maximum tenderness are the absolute worst. Those moments when my heart begins to soar – when Rosa first holds her arms out to me, when she kisses me wetly on the ear, when she wakes herself up by singing – those moments of bliss swoop straight into fear.

Some important part of emotional development must have passed me by. The bliss of Rosa's touch immediately transforms into fear. My intimate life is comprised of ugly new adjectival compounds: Tender-horror. Love-panic. Joystruck-grief.

I read about the science of feelings; I learn that different languages have different ways of articulating emotional experience. With a better vocabulary for complex feeling, one author argues, we might expand our understanding of our internal lives; we might lessen our panic at the un-parsable anomaly of our own feelings. The French, for example, use the term *l'appel du vide* – the appeal of the void – to describe the vertiginous pull at the edge of a precipice. It might have helped if I'd known this term, as I stood on Lendal Bridge seeing my baby fall. And then there's good old 'melancholy': Freud describes the melancholic losing the love object whilst it is still present. Perhaps these words would have helped me to navigate the grief of my love for Rosa.

Loving an infant requires a new vocabulary.

For instance:

If only. If only I'd done things differently. If only I'd enjoyed those early, never-again days and weeks with Rosa, knowing that she would still be here at the end of them. I rake my past for the failings that have brought me here. If only I'd planned the pregnancy. If only I'd been in a stable, loving relationship. If only I'd been able to stay with Sol. If only I had a functioning social *network*. If only my father hadn't been in the police – you pig's daughter, you scum of the earth. If only I could trust people. If only I did a different job. If only I didn't read the news. If only I'd learned how to mother – how to let the world mother me.

Later, I'll read my discharge notes, in which Francesca has written: *The patient was very anxious to know how long it would be before she felt better. She expressed high feelings of shame and failure for experiencing intrusive thoughts. She reported a pre-morbid personality of high achievement, goal setting and being always on the go.*

Pre-morbid personality. If only I hadn't been pre-morbid.

Loving an infant is ceaseless self-recrimination.

For instance:

Why am I trying to theorise like this? Francesca tells me that giving too much attention to my own thoughts is a symptom of my illness. Theorising is part of my problem, and a sign that I am still prone to over-interpreting the world. Loving Rosa has made me too alert to my passing cognitions and I've charged the images in my brain with premonitory power – reading my own thoughts like a bad literature student, analysing a Gothic novel and looking only for *foreshadowing*.

Loving an infant is my failure to accept the random.

When will I get better? For fuck's sake. Will I ever get better?

There is one last thing left on my list of fears: taking a train with Rosa. Francesca thinks I'm ready to go it alone; to bring the baby into proximity with speed and metal and bridges and high platforms and those sliding windows with the signs that tell you not to lean out because you'll be decapitated.

We are going to visit my mother.

At the station, I stand well back from the platform edge and then I step forward. I do not let myself count in any particular way that might save Rosa. When the train pulls in, a man offers to help me with the pram and I let him. It is nauseatingly unsteady when he lifts the front end. Inside, the movement of the train is also treacherous; lurching me left and right as I walk down the carriage with Rosa in my arms. We sit in a window seat and Rosa is super alert. She bangs one hand against the window and drools with delight. Yes, Rosa! Fields. Cows. Trees.

The colours are incredible: a long, lurid spill of late summer yellow as we draw closer to Leeds: fields of bright rape, irruptions of furze. Total colour drench. Rosa is transfixed.

An older woman boards the train at Micklefield. She sits across the aisle from me and asks how old Rosa is. Then she tells me about her own two children, who are grown up now. She tells me about her husband, who died of stomach cancer. Then the same cancer struck her son too. Her husband was dead within the year, but he didn't suffer. Her son, she says, he had done the suffering for both of them. He had survived it, so far, but his stomach was stapled to his spine.

All of this in less than ten minutes.

I remember Stacey's visit to York, that pale winter day before Rosa was born, when she told me about the eleven pregnancies she and her sister had carried. Five miscarriages and a stillbirth. I was affronted that Stacey had brought this up just before my due date. The word *stillbirth* had felt like a curse.

I know, now, that that conversation was an initiatory confidence. I couldn't face death back when I was pregnant. Not in the way that birth requires.

When Rosa needs to feed, I try to angle her towards the carriage window, but she wants to see the carriage and the people around us. She feeds in short bursts, rearing up, laughing goofily, milk spilling down her chin.

She is excited! To see clouds and sky and full green-yellow drench!

The velocity of the train lurches through my stomach. Let it all flood in: metal rushing tiny body tiny fragile body fontanelle screaming green fields rushing green.

Dewsbury and Batley blur past us: the start of the great drag of old industry through the valley bottoms – red-brick mills, boarded-up windows, fleets of white vans, a furnace chimney, rows of garages. The train cuts across the river as we near Huddersfield and then the valley opens wide, swathes of sunlight illuminating the great gas cylinders, the sprawl of the

ICI chemical plant, the stadium, the university; then the view
narrows again into blackened terraces, the town centre ware-
houses and sheet metal centres, the great sheds of Dunelm and
Lidl. Out the other side of town, and the embankment thickens,
arterial purple flowering through the undergrowth – foxgloves,
rhododendrons, buddleia, balsam. Drystone walls. Fields edged
with barbed wire. A pylon. A horse. A smashed-up greenhouse.
A patch of solar panels. A new-build estate, JCB stammering at
the bare earth. More, still more, of the detritus of industry, that
spill of defunct parts the whole length of the valley bottom from
Leeds to Manchester: sawtooth roofs, a new warehouse bolted
on to a sinking mill, a fleet of Fed Ex vans, a murder of crows
circling overhead, a long, broken sequence of Portakabins and
derelict sheds and garages. Above all this, rows of terraces zigzag
the valley side, golden stone smoked black; rising higher still,
Scapegoat Hill; the silhouette of the moortop, a stark black edge
against the summer sky.

It's a steep walk to my mother's house. We take the long ramp
from the station platform to the valley bottom, where the purple
balsam fills the canalside – a swathe of sweetly devouring newborn mouths. Then we track back up the valleyside, along rows of
terraces, until Mum's road is in sight.

I know that Tuesday is Mum's day off, but I have not told her
about our visit, for two reasons. First, in case I bottle it. Second,
so she doesn't have time to get fretful and bottle it herself. Her
replies to my messages have been intermittent, but she has sent
me something for Rosa almost every week – babygrows and bibs
and teething toys for her to chew – and I'm taking these gifts as
a good omen.

I stand on her doorstep. I've only been inside this house a handful of times: Mum bought it a decade ago with her partner, Mark. I knock on the door. Dogs bark on the other side. Mum works on reception at a veterinary practice in Halifax and she also volunteers at an animal shelter, which means she's always bringing home the animals that haven't been rehoused. *It's just for a bit*, she said the last time I visited, which was nearly two years ago, when a Dobermann attempted to clamber on to the couch and then on to my lap – *just till she's better and someone else can take her.* Mark had laughed. *Right*, he'd said. *We'll see, shall we?*

I hear movement on the other side of the door.

Quieten down, quieten down, my mother's voice is saying.

The door opens just a couple of inches.

Yes? my mum says.

Mum, I say, it's me.

Who, she says, Grace? Oh, my God. Are you OK?

Mum opens the door wider, and then a terrier is out on the pavement beside me, yapping at the pram.

Oh my God, oh my God, Mum says. Beardy! Get back in here. She yanks the dog inside. All the dogs barking behind her now.

Oh, Grace! I can't believe you're here, she says. Let me just go and put the dogs in the kitchen and then you can come in. If you want to?

While Mum fixes us some tea, I lift Rosa out of her pram and settle her on my lap. Rosa looks at our new surroundings with wonder. There is dog hair absolutely everywhere. But people have animals around babies all the time. Let the thoughts flood in. Suffocation on dog hair. That stuff in dog shit that makes kids go blind – toxoplasmosis. Rosa eating dog shit. Never leave a baby alone with a dog. A baby tossed in the air by a Pit Bull. Soft, warm, baby cheek, torn right through.

My mum comes back in from the kitchen, flushed and fretful.

I still can't believe it. That you're here, Grace. With the baby.

Mum can't sit still. She wrings her hands. I've hardly anything in, she says. Have you had your lunch?

We don't need anything, Mum, I say, I'll just give her a feed. And then you could hold her.

Oh, Mum says. Oh, she might not want to come to me. Don't make her. You're still feeding her? That's good. That's really good. Did they show you how to in the hospital?

Yes, I say. There was a kind midwife. She stayed with me that first night and showed me. I was lucky.

Yes, Mum says. Yes, that's good.

My mother sits down, but she's white-knuckled. Gripping the cuffs of her cardigan.

And how have you and Ryan been? Mum asks. Have things been OK?

I wasn't good at first, I say. I found things hard. Isobel stayed for a bit. It's getting better now, I say.

You're doing really well, Grace. I can tell just looking at you with that baby. So tuned into her. Knowing when she needs to be fed. I can tell you're doing brilliantly.

No, I say. Mum, I wasn't doing well. But I'm doing much better now. The doctor's been helping.

Mum stands up then. She turns away from me; looks like she might be about to bolt from the room.

It's my fault. You got this from me.

Mum, I say. Come and sit back down. Come on.

Just give me a minute. Give me a minute.

Mum has her hands on her own throat.

Fear of my mum dissolving; fear of my mum disappearing herself.

Don't make her come to me, Mum says. Don't make the baby come to me if she doesn't want to.

Come and sit down, Mum. Come and sit with us. Rosa doesn't care if you cry. She cries all the time. We both cry all the time.

Mum turns back towards me. Face flooded.

It's too much. I don't deserve to hold her.

Shhh, Mum, I say. Don't say that. It's not true.

One of the dogs is keening operatically in the kitchen.

Dad told us that our mother wasn't cut out for taking care of children – that mum couldn't hold us as babies. But on our contact visits, Mum used to hug us close in sudden desperate bursts. She would cling to us and start to shake and cry as she breathed into our hair. *Your nan will look after you much better than I ever could.* Perhaps she cared for us in the same terrible way that I first cared for Rosa. Perhaps she loved us with such wild panic that she had to leave us.

My mother is next to me on the sofa. I turn towards her with Rosa and Rosa looks at her with brimming-over alive-alive eyes. She oooh ooooohs and fans her hands rapidly, which is her new gesture of excitement. Then Rosa slaps one hand against my mum's chin.

Mum laughs.

Oh, you beautiful thing, she says. You beautiful thing.

My mother's hands are shaking when she holds them out to receive Rosa's tender body.

There are whole days now when I don't think of harm. Despite knowing that the world and everyone in it is chronically at risk, there are whole days when I remain in this shimmering thing called life.

At the end of that summer, we take a train to Brighton, three trains in fact, me and Rosa and Ryan-by-the-way. Rosa wears a ridiculous wide-brimmed sun hat and sees the sea for the first time, squinting and crying at the brightness of the light on the water, and we let her mouth a cone of chocolate ice cream and the coldness makes her zing with laughter.

We take Rosa to Ryan's old boat on the Thames, to visit his housemates, and Larry cooks soup for us, which we eat from scalding metal bowls. The lads tussle to hold Rosa and one of them plays peek-a-boo with her, Rosa's laugh coming in those hard short bursts.

We take Rosa to the park, and I feel the pleasure of being in the middle of a city in constant movement, the Minster bells pealing, the peregrines circling and shrieking in the sky. We set Rosa down on a blanket while the light moves through the leaves above us, and we open cans that Ryan has bought, and

Rosa's eyes are wide and rapturous as she stares towards the light.

I make a daily list of things for which I am grateful:

My appetite returning to me, prodigiously – for porridge thickened with cream and Guinness cake and salted cashews and sour noodles and citrus fruit

A voice-note from Isobel first thing in the morning

Neon yellow autumn leaves pockmarked with mould

The friendliness of dogs

Rosa's sleeping face: round and white and mushroom soft

A winter walk along the Foss – leaves perished from the willow trees, leaving a spill of bare yellow branches, illuminated in the cold sun; winter exposing the bright bones of life

Persephone Days – when winter is receding, and the daylight hours balance the darkness

A tulip coming up out of the ground, its leaves rolled together like a fat cigar

Catkins powdery with pollen

The nettles along the riverbank blistering back into flower

The honeyed scent of Rosa's scalp after shampooing

Rosa's eyes fluttering with pleasure as she falls asleep at my breast

Rosa meeting her own shadow on the wall, tracing it with her finger

Rosa eating fruit straight from my hands, licking my fingers clean

I am doing all the things that I'm supposed to do to take care of myself and my brain and my baby, and yet—

There are days with Rosa that are so bright – Rosa so lumi-
nously alive – I feel her as a wound. Then life becomes thin again.
I'll be terrified of the serrations of a carving knife. Of the roil of
boiling water in the kettle. I'm up in the small hours at my mother's house one long black night, soothing Rosa, who is feverish
and cutting teeth, and that expression – *cutting teeth*, meaning
the sharp eruption of bone through tender gums – will make
me think suddenly of the kitchen scissors downstairs. I'll see the
glinting blades, and the velocity with which they might move, and
the balance of everything will seem to hang in a second, and I'll
want to run then – I'll want to run with the blades all the way up
the valleyside, to bury them up on the moortop where the earth
swallows our secrets.

In the dead of night, back in the Valley, when the darkness sings
to me and I feel it through my body again, I don't know if Rosa
will ever be safe. Perhaps this realisation must bloom, eventually,
in all of us who are godless: that there is no system, no absolute
power that can keep us from harm. We are all of us in disorder. The
only pleasure from this world is the jolt of joyriding: the sudden,
hurtling, stolen thrill of our speed into the world, of not knowing
how long we will get away with it.

And there is so much surging pleasure to come: Somewhere
right now a child is being born and a mother is rapturous. The thick
lard of vernix gently towelled away, pulsing infant laid straight
on to her chest, her lips on the blood-soaked head, breathing the
baby in, oh, organ of mine. Right now, a child is being cradled in
warm water, her limbs unfurl, her mother's touch her first tender
sensation. Right now, an infant watches the pattern of light playing
through the leaves above, and the world is a hum and a whoosh and
a shriek in the air around her. Right now, a child rushes into the

sea, and gulps and screams at her first cold gush of ocean. A child chases a cat down the street, shrieking: Caaaat. A child buries her face in her mother's neck, then turns to her with a question, open and expectant as a flower seeking light. Mummy, can I eat the snow? Mummy, do we shrink when we die? Somewhere right now, a girl is learning the textures of heather and furze and how to follow the skylarks and meadow pipits, soaring up and over the most terrible and beautiful places.

And somewhere right now an infant is being harmed. All your worst fears are true, somewhere in this world. A baby is falling. A lighter rasps, singes against soft skin. The rain of mortar. Somewhere right now, a child's body is yielding to harm. Somewhere right now, an infant gulps once more for breath, then ceases her crying.

I let my fears flood me. I let my fears flood me over and over.

Alive. Alive. That is the pulse of your blood where it beats closest to the surface, in all the most tender places.

Acknowledgements

I am grateful for the work of W. H. Auden and Adam Phillips, quoted in the epigraphs to this novel. There are references throughout *raw content* to the writers I most loved as a young reader and aspiring writer: I am indebted to Annie Proulx, Daphne Du Maurier, Toni Morrison, Sylvia Plath, Irvine Welsh, Emily Brontë, and Jame Joyce. I am grateful for resources that have helped me to better understand OCD, in particular those provided by OCD-UK, which informed my discussion of 'scrupulosity' and historical figures associated with OCD. C. Purdon and D.A. Clark's study of 'Obsessive Intrusive Thoughts in Nonclinical Subjects' informed the list of common intrusive thoughts that features in the novel. Lisa Feldman Barrett's fascinating *How Emotions are Made: The Secret Life of the Brain*, inspired Grace's reflections on the new vocabulary required to love an infant.

My thanks to everyone at Corsair for treating this book with such care, and especially to Sarah Castleton for her faith, editorial brilliance and poetic ear. Deep thanks to my agent, Sabhbh Curran, for her immense patience and dedication. I am grateful for clever thoughts and encouragement from the following readers: Camilla Bostock, Abi Curtis, Kieran Devaney, Dulcie Few,

Thomas Houlton, Laura Joyce, Helen Jukes, Kate Murray-Browne, and Nicholas Royle. Conversations with friends sustained me through writing this book, and through the transitions that inspired it: thank you Alice Pelliccia-Bourke, Anne-Marie Evans, Clare Brook, Emma Phillips, Helen Pleasance, Janine Bradbury, Kaley Kramer, Kate Whittaker, Katy O'Neill, Kechi Ajuonuma, Kimberly Campanello, Liesl King, Lucy Rice, Nasser Hussain, Nathan Connolly and everyone at Dead Ink, Oliver Morgan, Rebecca Hawkins, Ruby Templeton, Sameer Rahim, Stu Hennigan, Sophie Nicholls, Sunjeev Sahota, and Sylvie Simonds. Dulcie Few needs thanking again: for being willing to talk about the most difficult things with total friendship and honesty.

Thank you to my mum and dad for their continual support; thank you, Michael and Betty, for making everything possible.

My deep gratitude for the work of two psychotherapists whose generosity, compassion, and insight helped light my way through the dark: Alex Lloyd and Lydia Noor, thank you.

Credits

James Joyce, *A Portrait of the Artist as a Young Man*, Penguin Modern Classics, 2000

C. Purdon and D.A. Clark, *Obsessive Intrusive Thoughts in Nonclinical Subjects* (1993), PubMed, National Center for Biotechnology Information <accessed 19th September 2024>: https://pubmed.ncbi.nlm.nih.gov/8257402/

OCDUK, *The history of OCD* <accessed 19th September 2024>: https://www.ocduk.org/ocd/history-of-ocd/

William Shakespeare, ed. intro. by Martin Wiggins, *Julius Caesar*, Penguin Classics, 2015

Lisa Feldman Barrett, *How Emotions are Made: The Secret Life of the Brain*, Macmillan, 2017